THE GIRL WHO TWEETED WOLF

HOBSON & CHOI SERIES

THE GIRL WHO TWEETED WOLF

RUSH JOBS

ISBN: 1500489859

ISBN-13: 978-1500489854

THE GIRL WHO TWEETED WOLF

HOBSON & CHOI – CASE ONE

NICK BRYAN

ONE
#HOBSONVSWOLF

Not only was there no name stencilled on the window of Hobson's office door, it didn't even have a window. Angelina was disappointed – what kind of crappy detective doesn't have an office name stencil window?

Instead, it was a solid beige fire door. The only thing marking it out from the beige corridor was the change in texture from beige plaster to beige wood. Same old London office in a boring building. Clearly all her effort to dress interesting had been silly. The black floaty layers and purple tights looked ridiculous against all the nothingness.

Too late to change though, she was already five minutes late. She knocked on the hollow, cheap-sounding door, with the firmness of an adult, rather than a nervous sixteen-year-old. Or so she hoped.

"Yeah, come in," said the hoarse yell from inside.

Angelina pushed the door open. Considering how long she'd spent staring at the tedious thing, it floated away easily.

The office behind was more interesting than the corridor, thankfully. Bright blue, two desks, a few filing cabinets. But no discarded whiskey bottles, nor a mattress round back where the detective slept.

"Good morning, Choi," said a deep voice. The huge man behind the larger desk leapt up, revealing a pressed black suit and straight tie. Buttoned down to a fault, this guy could be a real veteran police detective, right up to the grey peppering his short dark hair.

And why was he calling her by surname?

"Good to meet you. I'm John Hobson, just *Hobson* is fine though." And, when she didn't immediately reply: "How are you? Good trip over?"

"Um, thanks, I'm fine, you too." She forgot to punctuate any of that, blushing as soon as it finished.

"Good. Good. Well, welcome to our new work experience internship programme. I hope I'll be able to show you something about the business in two weeks. As you can see, I've cleared a desk for you here." He gestured at the smaller one in the room, with a wedge of papers recently shoved to one end.

"Looks nice," she glanced down and nodded. "Lots of room."

Another silence.

"So," he was already standing up and hooking his jacket off the back of the chair, "I have to get moving for a lunch meeting, but I do have a job for you to get on with."

Her ears pricked up, but expectations remained measured. She'd be filing all those papers away, wouldn't she? Or running out to buy milk?

"I've noticed this social Twitter internet media thing seems to be taking off," he said, gesturing widely at the computer on her desk, as if that explained everything, "could you create an account for me and get me some of those… followers?"

Angelina blinked. "I'm sorry?"

"Well, you know. I've just repainted my office, I want to be modern, and your lot seem to be familiar with this kind of thing."

"My *lot*? What do you mean *my lot*?"

"No no no no *no*," Hobson spun round, nearly whirling her across the room, "not Asians. Teenage girls."

"Oh. Right." Depressingly, she was relieved he'd even noticed she was Asian. "Well, sure. I'll see what I can do."

"Thanks, Choi." He shrugged his massive coat on, composure back in place. "Just a couple of hundred should do. Cheers, running late, back in an hour."

With that, he waved and dashed out the door. And then popped his head back round. "Oh, could you also go to the shops and get some coffee? Ain't much left."

Angelina nodded, and kept her sigh inside until he'd definitely gone. This office was the size of a rich person's cupboard.

Picking up the coffee took a few minutes. The hardest part was checking out his machine and working out what type to buy. Now she was an intern, Angelina knew she had to do these menial tasks, so swallowed her pride and went to Tesco.

Not long after, guzzling a pack of dirt-cheap cardboard crisps, she plonked herself down in front of her computer. She had a job to do, so resisted the urge to head straight for Facebook and complain about her negligent boss.

Instead she went on Twitter and got to work. She typed, she schmoozed, she strived, she read blog posts about *Social Media Success*, many of which made her angry. Finally, several tweets and retweets later, something clicked.

Shortly later, so did the door to their office, as Hobson returned. His *lunch meeting* ended at a reasonable time and left him completely sober; again, both reassuring and disappointing. When did she get to sniff corpses and snort whiskey, delve deep into the underworld?

Instead, she had a presentable, clean shaven, punctual detective without a visible drinking problem. Should've been more specific on the form.

"So Choi," Hobson said, his jacket flopping back over the chair, "am I… *trending* yet?"

He pronounced *trending* like it was the name of an alien planet.

"Um, sort of," she said.

"Sort of?"

"Well, you've got 353 followers…" Angelina broke off mid-stream as a rectangular email notification popped up. "Well, 354 now. But I had to say some stuff to get them."

Hobson fiddled with his own computer, not paying much attention. "Yeah? What kind of stuff?"

"I tried just creating an account and following people, engaging with other detectives, but it wasn't working much," she could hear herself talking faster in response to his blank stares, "so I found an interesting murder case and said that if you got enough followers, you'd totally solve it for free."

And it sounded like a better idea at the time, she added silently, rolling her chair away from Hobson as his face turned red and he stood up, tie flapping wild. It was hard not to be scared when a man bigger than the room he was sitting in started yelling at you.

"You did *what?*" At least he'd noticed her. "Do you have you any idea how shitty that is? What if the press find out? What if the victim's family find out? How do you know I even *can* solve it? How am I meant to pay my rent?"

"I don't know, I'm sorry, I wanted to get it right and I just..." Angelina inhaled deep and snorted by accident. "I may have said something else too."

"Oh God."

"Yeah. If we get up to 400 followers, you have to fight a wolf."

The email indicator leapt up again. Only forty-five to go.

With a speed you wouldn't expect from a man of his size, Hobson turned off her monitor, and pointed to the tiny space in front of his main desk.

"Go on, Choi." He jabbed the finger again. "Plant yourself there and go over what the hell's going on. Quick as you like."

"Well, um, you know Twitter?"

"No."

"Right."

To her relief, the phone on his desk rang, but her respite was short-lived. Hobson picked it up, listened for a few seconds, then said "Yup, no comment," and beeped the handset off again.

"Choi. You were saying?"

"Well," she took a deep breath, knowing this was her moment, "I just started an account, and it wasn't going that well, and then I had this idea and I started up a hashtag, it was *#HobsonVsWolf* which I thought was pretty good, and then people started getting really into it and…"

Hobson held up a hand, eyes tightening as if suffering the beginnings of a headache. "Okay. Pretending for a moment that I know what a hashtag is – people really went for this? You suggested I fight a wolf and that was it?"

"Well, a couple of people thought it was insensitive, but mostly, they seemed really keen. We were even at the bottom of the UK trending topics for a few minutes! So you see," she finished, determined to end on a high, "I did exactly what you asked for."

Angelina was sure his head raised up for a few moments when she mentioned the trending, twitching like a dog who'd smelt some appealing food. However, his disapproving scowl soon reasserted itself.

"Okay, so I think we've gone as far as we can with the *how*. Can we move on to why you thought this was a good idea?"

Dragging out an inhale to collect her thoughts, Angelina gave it a go. "I don't know if you've done much research into online marketing and social media in the past, Mister Hobson…"

"I told you Choi, just Hobson, it's fine."

Soon, Angelina thought, he might ask permission to call her *Choi*. Somehow, he made her name alone sound racist. But this wasn't the time to file a complaint.

"Okay, well, *everyone else* has been online for quite some time," she said. "You see, you have to engage with people in a way they understand, a way that's funny and catches their interest."

"Right…"

"So what I was doing, I think, is trying to make you seem relevant and exciting. You know, like someone who gets up and solves crime, instead of just going to lunch and sounding bored. Tap into modern events in a way that draws attention to your business. Like '*Hello, you've all got this problem and I, John Hobson, am the solution! I fight the bad guys! I'll protect you from the wolf!*' Because everyone loves Sherlock Holmes or whoever, so you've got to be that guy. You see?"

"Sounds shallow and awful." Hobson shook his head. "Honestly, Choi, you kids watch too much television."

Her eyes were stuck open. Why wasn't he excited by any of this?

Speech seemed pointless in the face of grand apathy. The skies outside greyed over, no doubt in sympathy at the boring office nightmare she was trapped in. So much for her plan to tease friends doing office admin placements – she might call them up and beg for spare desks.

And then another phone rang. Hobson reached back, rustled around in the tiny space behind his desk and plucked a brown, dusty wired receiver out of nowhere. Had the decency to mutter "Internal line" at her before talking into it.

"Hello? Hi Will, what's up? Delivery?"

It all snapped into place, as Angelina remembered Will, the good-looking receptionist she'd met on the way up. She'd thought he ought to be older, or at least scarier, to be the front desk guy in such a dodgy block.

Hobson was still talking. "You saw what on Twitter? Oh, um, yeah, I guess that is us."

"No, I'm not going to fight a wolf, my work experience girl got a little carried away." He laughed into the phone, still somehow sounding bored at the same time. "But yeah, it's an interesting case, isn't it? I guess it captured our imagination. Well, you know, I don't want to tell you too much this early in the investigation, but keep watching the Twitters, I suppose."

Well, Angelina stewed, this internship was meant to prepare her for the world of work – now she knew how it felt when the boss took credit for her effort.

"Yup," he continued, "I suppose that was in bad taste, I'll have a word with Choi about overstepping the mark in future."

Now she was the heartless bitch too. Her hand flicked, wanting to grab the phone and apologise to Will personally.

"Okay, thanks for calling, Will. Cheers."

He replaced the handset, slowly. Tapped his desk. Eventually looked up at Angelina.

"So, real people can see your tweeting?"

"Real people?"

"Real real people? Like Will downstairs? Real people as opposed to internet people and trolls and whatnot?"

"Yes, Mister Hobson, the people on the internet are definitely real."

"Interesting." On that, he stood up, flicking his coat from the back of the chair. "Suppose we'll take a look at this murder, then. You can brief me on the way."

Hobson was moving across the tiny office, barely leaving room for her to stay standing. Determined to go with the flow, Angelina grabbed her own jacket and headed for the door behind him.

"Hey, Hobson, um, do we have to walk out past the main reception desk? The one where… Will sits?"

"Yes, that's the front door."

"Can we maybe use a back door?"

"Why?"

"Never mind."

TWO
DRY BLOOD

There was a *lot* of police tape on Markham Road. Far more than she'd ever expected. Angelina stood outside the two houses, staring at the shiny web criss-crossing and peeling off their porches. No sign of any policemen or police cars, smashed in front doors or blood seeping under them, but yellow tape? Yeah, a *lot* of that.

She glanced at Hobson. "So, um, we just knock?"

"Let's get this clear now – *I am not Batman.*"

"No no, I just mean…" She gulped as a gaggle of men moved closer – a cliché of a tabloid reporter, cloned. "Isn't this a bit insensitive? Turning up at their house like this?"

"Heh." Hobson chuckled and kicked the garden gate open. "Should've thought of that before you put them on the internet as a freebie really, Choi."

Without pausing, he swept the tape aside with one huge arm and strode up to the door in his black suit like a visiting undertaker, knocking so hard Angelina saw it shake. She chased along behind him, the assembled journalists turning towards the noise like a flock of birds.

"Hobson, with all the tape, doesn't that mean..."

"Oh, they're in."

A rustling behind the door, a crunch in its frame as someone inside leaned forward to look through the peephole. Behind them in the road, definite camera clicks. At least someone appreciated her amazing first-day outfit, Angelina thought, hoping the guy would open up before the paps asked her a question.

"Don't get excited, Choi," Hobson said, "we may not get in right away, might have to negotiate through the door, exchange numbers and call them later..."

The entrance swung open, to reveal a man with crimson gelled hair and oddly wide eyes. He was wearing a baggy hoodie, jeans and a huge grin, considering the murder in his house.

"Hey!" he said. "You're the internet guys! I saw your hashtag! Hobson, right?"

Angelina flashed a smug grin at her boss but he faced forward.

"Yeah, that's me. This is my assistant Angelina Choi," awkward wave from her, poking a hand out behind Hobson, "we wondered if we could speak to you about the murders?"

"Wow, you're actually investigating? I assumed that was just shitty online marketing."

Only then did Hobson return Angelina's smirk, before turning back to the resident. "We are looking into it. Can we come in, mister...?"

"Oh, yeah, Ric McCabe, hi." Broad wave, before looking past them to the photographers barely keeping off the front garden. "Best get inside, it's a jungle out there."

Ric ushered them in and slammed the door; Angelina was pretty sure he gave a middle finger to the waiting hordes before it fully closed.

Inside, all was dark; dim light and faded walls combined to blanket them with a sickly yellow glow. There were no windows, just a couple of heavy fire doors to the right and a staircase up to a world of darkness. It was about as homely as prison; she missed her mother's flowery wallpaper.

"Nice place," Hobson nodded, sincere as ever, "looks very secure."

Ric just laughed. "You mean aside from the dead housemate?"

"Obviously. Speaking of which, I'm told it happened in the kitchen?"

"Wow, you're a cheery fun guy." Ric looked over to Angelina. "Isn't he fun? With his serious face and his funeral suit."

"Thanks," Hobson said, not letting her speak. "You're quite cheery and fun yourself, considering your housemate's just been ripped to shreds by a wolf."

"Well," Ric said, "we never liked him."

Not letting them digest that, Ric pushed open the second of the two doors on the right, and they entered a dingy living room. It had a window, at least, although enclosed by overhanging neighbours to stop too much light reaching it. There were two dusty sofas, a small TV and one used breakfast bowl on the table.

Commanding attention above those things was another mess of police tape around the closed door at the back. That must be the kitchen. A smear of red slipped beneath the crack of this door, and she could see more reflecting behind it, clotting and dark. That packet of cheap crisps stirred inside her.

"Hobson..." She said his name without meaning to. At least she hadn't called him "Daddy".

He glanced over at her, kept his face immobile but seemed to register something. Was she turning green, like a cartoon character?

"Mister McCabe," he said, "has the mess from the murder been cleaned up yet?"

"Afraid not," he sighed, "they make you do it yourself, did you know that? The cops cart off your mate's body, then you have to either scrub his guts up, or pay through the nose to get a crime scene cleaner in."

"What, seriously?" Angelina said. "They just leave them there?"

"I know, it's a fucking disgrace isn't it? I mean, it's not as if I killed him."

"Thanks for clarifying, Mister McCabe. So you haven't called a cleaner?"

"Well, y'know," Ric said, "it took us long enough to arrange a guy when the washing machine packed up."

"I can probably recommend someone if it'll help."

"We're kinda hoping the landlord will take care of it, to be honest."

"I see. You say *we*, is the other housemate in?"

"Pete, no, think he's at work. Do you want to question him and stuff?"

"Would be nice to have a word. But I should probably look at your kitchen first."

The thought of hard blood left untouched on a kitchen floor was scabbing over Angelina's thoughts, but instead of wrenching the door open this time, Hobson turned to her.

"Choi," he said, pulling out his wallet, "saw a Subway up the road, could you get me a meatball sub? Brown bread, no onions, coke. And whatever you want too." He thrust a ten pound note at her.

She wasn't sure whether to be thrilled or disappointed. "But… what about…"

"I've asked my friends and they say this is what interns are for. Get the sandwich. Mister McCabe can talk me through the murder. You've read up already, it'll be boring for you."

Telling herself it was fair enough, Angelina nodded. She took the money, turned and headed out the door with a wave, pulling her hood up to deter the paparazzi. It was unlike her to be conflicted about the prospect of a free Subway – last time her Mum had offered to buy one, she'd danced two full circuits around the living room.

As soon as she popped her head outside, the flashing and clicking started, but died down when they realised it was just some little girl. She sighed and headed back the way they came.

Must try not to look too hard at the meatball sandwich with globs of tomato sauce, in case it reminded her of crushed guts.

"Seriously, Mister Hobson, you sure you're a detective?" McCabe was facing the other way when he said it, so chanced a clever-clever smile. Hobson saw his smug face reflected in the living room window. "Because based on the suit, you'd be better off as an insurance salesman."

"Right. Thanks." Hobson ignored him and kept listening for the front door slam. He was old enough not to care about awkward silences – in fact, you could get a lot out of people by riding them longer.

The crash sounded, and Choi was gone. No shuffling to indicate she'd faked her exit to listen in. Time to get to work, then.

"Okay then, Mister McCabe," he indicated the still-closed kitchen door with his entire hand, not even bothering to point with a specific finger, "let's see the crime scene."

"Um, sure." McCabe said, suddenly shy. "Of course."

More squeamish panic? Should he send McCabe off to pick him up some cake? He settled for an angry glare. McCabe was skinny and defensive, he'd bow down to sheer size.

Sure enough, Ric's hand went straight to the door handle. It swung open to reveal, at long last, the scene of a brutal murder. It was a kitchen, the kind Hobson hadn't lived with since his *very* early twenties – a few plates which obviously rotated on and off the drying rack, rusty cutlery, one browned-to-death baking tray, barely enough space to swing any pet, even a hamster.

However, it turns out there *was* enough room for a dog to maul an adult male to death with tooth and claw. They'd removed the whole body – few police were cartoonishly incompetent enough to leave a stray finger behind – but the blood splashed far and wide, dribbling towards the entrance down a slight incline in the floor.

It spattered down the fridge, rendering the magnetic poetry illegible, seeped into the loaf of half–chopped bread on the side, forming a new dark crust. Even with afternoon light flooding in, it was a defiled, scabby mess. Hobson couldn't even find an unbloodied spot of floor to step inside.

"So," Hobson said, "could you walk me through what happened here?"

"Well," Ric said, "in case it wasn't obvious, my housemate William was ripped apart by some sort of huge dog or wolf or whatever. Maybe a fox, I hear they've been trying to get into our houses and eat our babies for years now. Or that's what the newspapers say anyway."

McCabe snorted with laughter, Hobson refused to smile.

"Thanks," he said, voice flat. "But maybe some more detail?"

"Do I actually have to go stand in the blood and walk it through? Because these are new shoes."

"Just shut the fuck up and get on with it," Hobson said, feeling his fingers twitch.

"At the same time? Because..."

"Mister McCabe. *Now*, please."

"Right."McCabe gulped and continued. "Okay. So I was out, came home and the police were all over my house."

"Out where?"

"Pub. So turns out, William – that's the dead one – had been in the kitchen making tea, when someone kicked the back door in, looks like, and let his dog in to do the dirty work."

Tired of being dainty, Hobson ground his boots into the blood and entered. The clots sent up a thin red dust, but he'd stood in worse than that. Sure enough, the back door lock was smashed, didn't even shut properly anymore. Only a plastic mop bucket on the floor kept it in place.

"So someone let the dog in."

"Well, yeah," McCabe said. "Unless it was a fucking werewolf, I suppose. It smashed through the fence in the garden," he pointed towards the back of the house, "and around the same time it killed our neighbour on the other side too."

"Yeah, the other guy." Hobson stroked his chin. Looked down and saw a couple of red flaky pawprints pointing towards the back door.

Without asking permission, he kicked the mop bucket away, sending it scraping through the blood to a halt, then tugged the door open and stepped out.

A thin pathway led alongside the house, weeds sprouting between paving stones and in all other gaps. A few bloody smears next to the doorstep, and after that not a drop, never mind a pawprint.

"Someone picked it up," he murmured.

"Yeah, but they can't find it," McCabe continued. "No sign of it here or next door, and all the doors were shut."

Hobson ignored the idiot and swept up the garden, glancing over to the afore-mentioned hole in the fence. It looked like it'd been knocked through from the other side.

No obvious blood stains out here, although he'd struggle to spot them among all the mud and overgrown plants anyway. Unfortunately, the pavement finished, and all that remained was a jungle of tall grass and attacking foliage, snaking up then falling back down again. Still, that meant you could see a clear, blood-free trail of stamped-down plantlife where the dog had scythed through the garden.

Hobson nodded to himself, just as McCabe caught back up.

"Right. And you said you didn't like the victim?" Hobson said, with another firm look.

"Well." McCabe paused over his answer. "He was a sulky, difficult, messy guy. Not many people did. He worked with my other housemate, no-one at their office really liked him either."

"Right, thanks. And the other housemate's at work right now?"

"Pete? Yeah."

Hobson gave a polite smile, which he only ever granted someone once their audience was at an end. "Good. Just give me the address of that company and I'll leave you be for now."

When Hobson emerged back onto Markham Road, Choi was already coming the other way, munching on one sandwich and carrying the other in a bag. She dawdled at first, but picked up speed once she noticed him.

"Choi." Appreciative nod. "Thanks for the food. Come on, we're off to meet some trendy brats."

"What?" she said, almost spinning in place.

"Some social media marketing company in East London. Dead guy and third housemate both worked there, I'm told not many of them liked him. Maybe they whipped an envelope round the office to fund a hitman."

"Oh." She looked back at the two taped-up houses and small group of photographers in front of them. "Aren't we going to look at where the other guy was killed?"

"Not yet," Hobson said. "He lived alone, and I ain't

breaking in with the paparazzi watching."

"Right." Choi nodded, probably trying not to seem relieved. "So what did you make of that guy Ric?"

"Massive wanker."

"Think he did it?"

"Probably not."

"Why?"

"I'm just never that lucky."

THREE
SOCIAL AWESOME

"So it's not an office block?" Hobson took another look at the mess of conjoined rectangles across the road. "Because it looks a lot like one to me."

"No," Choi read out from its website on her needlessly expensive phone, "according to this, the Inspiration Gestation Station is a shared space where ideas can thrive."

"I see."

The duo sat in a stained café, down the road from the idea-pod in question. If they were going to enter that hellish new age pit of self-love, Hobson had insisted, they were damn well going to collect their thoughts in a proper greasy spoon first, rather than the heavily upholstered coffee house Choi wanted.

This being shitty East London, of course, it took an eternity to even find an acceptable café.

"So why are we here?" she said. "Shouldn't we be investigating the dodgy neighbour with the attack dog?"

"No. That isn't the interesting part, Choi. Someone went to the trouble of kicking the door in to kill William Lane. That means motive, and it looks like half his life is in that shitheap over there."

"And what are we waiting for?" Choi glanced across the road. "It'll be the end of the day soon."

"That's the trick, Choi," Hobson said. "Or my trick, at least. Catch people late enough in the day that they're relaxing, but not so late they've started going home."

She started tapping at her phone again – Hobson almost made a sharp comment about texting while the boss was talking, until he realised she was writing down what he'd said.

So he gave her a second to finish, draining his tea from the no-longer-white cup.

"Shall we go?" He pointed at the Inspiration Gestation Station, determined not to speak its name out loud. "Think we're in the right time zone now."

"Sure thing!" Choi slipped her phone away and leapt upwards at once, taking another nervous glance at nearby tables. A couple of the stares were lingering on the kid; maybe he'd been too successful in making her uncomfortable.

Shooting a glare at one particularly lascivious middle-aged man, he swept her out to the street. Considering how uncomfortable the Hipster Box Station was about to make him feel, hopefully karma would balance out.

Hobson had never been famous. People rarely recognised him in the streets, and the ones who did either ran away or punched him. So it still came as a shock when he entered the Inspiration Gestation Station, and the receptionist's eyes widened before the door even fell shut.

The foyer itself, behind the bland-looking glass door, was full of brightly coloured geometric shapes, murals of white-and-yellow flowers, TV monitors and a couple of vending machines. It was like a playground area for tall children. Hobson scowled at it all – Choi was grinning widely.

"Mister Hobson?"

The receptionist herself was a tiny, cutesy thing with long curly hair – the curveless figure of a cocktail stick and the dress sense of My Little Pony. Hobson didn't like to rule anyone out at this early stage, but she might not be the killer.

He paced across the horrible green flooring – fucking Christ, was this fake grass? – and shook her tiny hand in his enormous one. "Hi, John Hobson. Nice to meet you. You've seen us on…" Reluctant pause. "On the *tweets*, I suppose?"

"I'm Jacqueline Miller – everyone calls me Jacq – yes I saw you on Twitter – I can't believe what happened to William, you'll catch the killer won't you?"

"No, yeah. Just getting started right now, we're here to talk to the victim's colleagues."

And oh Lord, Hobson thought, they've painted the sun on the blue walls, above the flowers and the actual fucking astroturf. This was the pasture of his nightmares.

"Of course, so you want to go up to Social Awesome on the third floor."

"Social Awesome." Hobson sighed. "I suppose so. Do I need to sign in somewhere?"

"Yes, Mister Hobson," she pulled out a clipboard, "then you can head up to Social Awesome."

"Can't *wait*."

He snatched the pen.

Without waiting for orders like she should, Choi decided it was her turn to question Jacq. He'd thought she was content staring at the awful murals. "So, um, you knew William Lane?"

"Not really, I mean, I just work down here at reception," she said, "but we talked, I suppose, sometimes, about stuff."

"And he didn't, like, say anything to you?" Choi said.

"He never said much." Jacq shook her head. "I'm sure he had his own problems, I don't want to be mean about him when he's only been dead a couple of days."

"What," Choi said, "problems like drugs? Or running a brothel?"

Hobson signed his name in a scrawl, then cut in. "What my *intern* meant to say was: did William Lane seem troubled at all in the last few days?"

"No, well, he had been leaving sooner after work, but these guys often have to go to parties and stuff, so I just thought, you know, busy. He was about the same as he ever was. He did, um, well…"

Hobson smacked the guest clipboard over to Choi, almost winding her. "Yes?"

"He'd been on a date with my friend Emily not that long ago. It didn't work out, but nothing bad, just didn't work. Can't believe he's gone, she was only talking about him the other day."

"I see."

"And she also works upstairs, so, y'know, maybe it had been awkward. Still, I can't believe they would... you know, I just saw him a few days ago."

"Bloody hell. Right."

Choi finished off the form, and Hobson pointed at the huge double doors off to the right, with man-sized daisies painted on them. "Is *thi*s the lift?"

"Yes! Press for the third floor."

"Thanks."

"No problem! Hope you catch the bad guys!"

Jacq managed a wide smile, which Hobson and Choi returned awkwardly until the lift closed over their rictus faces.

"So, Hobson, think *she* did it?"

"Will you be asking me this whenever we meet anyone?"

"Did she, though?"

"Probably not, but hard to trust anyone *that* twee, innit?"

After a day spent in a tiny office, a dark house and a stinking café where fat stubbly men stared at her and licked their lips, Angelina felt pure joy when she saw the offices of Social Awesome.

The foyer area was fun enough, with its field motif and cheerful sheep murals. She'd seen Google's offices in pictures and always liked their primary coloured amazingness. She liked the sound of that working day too: sit on a cylindrical bean bag during meetings, look through a wall made of glass, play on-site table-tennis at lunch, deliver an inspirational talk on YouTube afterwards.

Upstairs, in Social Awesome itself, everything was clean! Open-plan! Freshly assembled wooden furniture! Office chairs with wheels! White boards with **TWITTER STRATEGY** at the top! Enough employees to be busy yet unintimidating!

No, Social Awesome didn't solve murders, but so far, Angelina wasn't blown away by the glamorous world of detective work.

Angelina and Hobson took a few steps into Social Awesome, and a red-haired woman in dishevelled business casual noticed them. She seemed pissed off about looking away from her computer, and seeing the guests responsible only made it worse.

"Hey, are you Hobson?" she said.

Hobson didn't help by sighing. "Yes, I am. And you are?"

"I'm Lettie Vole, I'm office manager here," she got up from her seat, striding around the desk to shout at them, "and you vultures can *fuck off* back where you came from."

"Okay, look, Ms Vole, we're just trying to..." Hobson began.

"Pick up Twitter followers from William's murder? Look, he may have been a bit of a nob, but he was *our* nob, and I'm not going to let you cash in. You're like those lawyers on the TV, telling people they could claim a huge pay-out from the accident they had."

There was a pause. Angelina almost blurted out a tearful apology, but Lettie Vole continued: "Only worse, because at least *those* accidents aren't fatal since people are still alive to claim on them."

That seemed to be it. Hobson didn't have much to say, although he did give Angelina one of the now-familiar *I Told You So* glares.

"Look, Lettie," Angelina said at last. "I'm really sorry, I was just trying to…"

She was on the verge of crying now. Not how she'd wanted her first day to go. Between Lettie shouting and her own high-pitched squeaks, the other four people in the office couldn't help but watch.

"I'm sorry, okay? I'm the one who did the Twitter thing." She was dying on her feet. "Hobson was just humouring me because it's my first day. We'll go."

"Sorry," said a voice from off to one side, "I couldn't help but overhear – that was *your* Twitter strategy?"

Wiping her eyes with the back of her hand, Angelina looked round. There was a guy there, casual shirt, same shade of red hair as Lettie, small pointy face. "Um, I guess," she said. "Don't know if it was exactly a strategy."

He gave her a patronising smile. "Well, if it helps, it was pretty good. I'm Pete, I'm an account executive here, and an unknown brand picking up followers at that speed gave us all something to think about. Don't get me wrong, it was in terrible taste, but y'know, what *is* taste, nowadays?"

He gestured at Lettie. "Excuse my sister, she likes to shout and swear."

"That's okay." Angelina nodded at said sister, but Lettie was busy narrowing her eyes at her brother, as if hoping he'd be the next person shredded by a wolf.

Something here seemed to reignite Hobson's interest. "Sorry," he leaned in, "you're Pete?"

"Pete Vole, yeah," he said, "have we met?"

"No, but I spoke to your housemate Ric, he said you all worked together here."

"Yeah, I guess that's true."

"Excuse me," Lettie said, "are we actually letting them do this, then? Exploit Will's death for pageviews?"

"Oh, well." Pete paused. "I was just trying to stop you making this little girl cry."

"So," Lettie continued, "I can kick them out? As long as I don't upset that one?"

"Actually, Pete has a point." A tall man joined the conversation now. "I'd like to have a chat with you, Mister Hobson."

The newcomer was long, thin, almost skeletal, and wearing a skinny suit that emphasised it. When his gaunt face smiled, the skin stretched. Angelina wondered how old he was – could be in his thirties, could easily be someone's great-grandfather.

"I'm Edward Lyne," he continued, "the owner of Social Awesome, and I think we could be of use to each other."

His voice was totally accentless – snuck under your skin, slithered in your ears. Angelina glanced at Hobson for reassurance, but he wasn't taking his eyes off Edward Lyne.

"Nice to meet you, Mister Lyne," Hobson smiled, unblinking, and went through yet another handshake. "What did you want to chat about?"

"First off, I'd like to do it in my office," Lyne said, gesturing to a small box in the corner. Clearly only the boss got his own walls. Inside, darkness, filing cabinets and a single desk. "I'm sure Peter and Violet can look after your young friend."

Angelina simmered. Why did everyone here treat her like a schoolgirl? These people were meant to be Awesome! But no, just some angry ginger siblings and the missing link between Jack Skellington and Lord Voldemort.

"Choi," Hobson risked looking away from Lyne to give her instructions. "Have a chat with these nice people, especially the ones we haven't met yet, ask about William. Looks like I'm going to have a word with Mister Lyne."

"No sweat, Hobson!" she said. Maybe the thumbs up had been overkill.

"Kids nowadays." With a shake of his head, Hobson gestured towards Lyne's corner office. "Okay, I'm all yours."

Inside Edward Lyne's office, with the door shut, the darkness rushed forward to envelop them both. It wasn't quite nighttime, but the evening had advanced a hell of a lot since Hobson and Choi entered the Inspiration Desperation Plantation. Hobson didn't scare easily – after all, he was bigger than everyone – but seeing Lyne's thin frame in silhouette put him in mind of a rearing skeletal scorpion.

"So, Mister Hobson, that really was one hell of a social media strategy."

From the expectant grin on Lyne's white face, Hobson suspected he was being buttered up. "Glad you liked it, Mister Lyne. Some people seem to find it distasteful."

"Ah, you mean our office manager Miss Vole?" he said.

"For example."

Lyne shrugged, the outline of his shoulders rising and falling clearly in the darkness. "She runs the office but she isn't really part of what we do. The truth of the matter is: your methods might be unconventional, but we think it flagged you up as a company we could really do business with."

"Because we have a Twitter account?"

"Everyone has a Twitter account, Mister Hobson."

Hobson laughed out loud. "I don't."

"Even if you bring in some little Asian girl to type the updates, it's *you* as far as the world is concerned."

Hobson ignored the racism to keep things moving. "Okay. I gotta say, Lyne, you're not what I expected as the owner of a company called 'Social Awesome'."

"You thought I'd wear bermuda shorts to work and own four smoothie makers?"

"Something like that."

"Because the company brand speaks louder than what's inside it, Mister Hobson. Just look at your Twitter account."

"Touché," Hobson growled.

The conversation rolled to a stop, blackness crept further down the wall.

"So, Mister Hobson, I thought I'd save you any future embarrassing conversations about your motives. I'm taking you on formally to investigate my dead employee, how does that sound?"

"Right." Mustn't seem too keen. "Why?"

"Because, as I say, I think you might be our kind of company."

"If you're talking about Twitter," Hobson said, "you need to take that up with my intern."

"Maybe I'll have a chat with her later." Lyne accompanied that with a smile and full flash of his gums. A surprise to discover there was *any* flesh in there.

"Maybe." Not a chance in Hell.

"So you accept?"

"Yes, but obviously it'll be expensive."

Not to mention: damn sight easier to investigate with a legitimate reason to be involved.

"That's fine. I'll get Lettie to send over the paperwork, you fill in your rate and I'll sign it off as long as you're not taking advantage."

"Suppose I'll get to work, then."

He stood up before Lyne could say anything, and reached across for the handshake. Seconds later, he cut it off, unsettled by how thin the other man's skin felt.

"So," Pete said as soon as Hobson shut that door behind him, "want me to introduce you to Emily and Matt?"

"Who?" Angelina's eyes darted about.

"Those two?" He indicated the remaining Social Awesome employees: a suited woman with a blonde bob and a man in a hoodie, a mess all over. "The ones your boss told you to talk to?"

"Oh." He was smiling at her again, wasn't he? Was it because she'd cried in front of him? "I… yes, I guess?"

She saw Pete's sister blasting her brother with the worst glare yet. Pretending not to notice, Angelina made her way across the open-plan mass of desks to that corner, near a huge window and a full whiteboard. There was a similar board in Hobson's office, with writing left so long, it wouldn't wipe off.

In front of it, at a workstation drowning in used notepaper, the guy in the hoodie wasn't looking up at her. What was his name?

"Hi?" Angelina said, waving. "Matt?"

He remained motionless, as if hoping she meant someone else.

From behind her, the woman with the hair called out. *"Hey, Matt!"*

He twitched, but not quick enough. A biro arced over Angelina's shoulder and clattered onto Matt's spacebar, he jumped backwards with a yell. As his head whiplashed from the desk, tiny earphones dropped out from under his messy hair and fell away.

Once his chair rolled to a stop, he sat for a second, before looking past Angelina. "Emily?"

"Sorry," came Emily's voice, "I think the little detective wants to talk to you."

"Hi, yes, thanks." Angelina moved towards the window to get out of the crossfire. "Hi, I'm Angelina, looking into William's murder. I was wondering if either of you knew who might've done it?"

Her two interviewees stared at her – maybe a real detective would've used a more subtle, insidious and probing question?

Emily cracked first: "Well, I went on a date with him a couple of weeks ago, it was awkward but not so awkward I'd kill him."

"Oh, okay. That's good. But why did you do that?"

"What do you mean?"

"Well…" Angelina said, "no-one seems to like him, so why did you date him?"

"Because he was funny, because I only met him three months ago when I started here, he seemed interesting, and lastly, because it's none of your business."

"Well, like I said, we're…"

"Looking into it, yes. Who hired you to do this, exactly? Are the police subcontracting?"

Angelina snapped. "Because it's our job, and we want to. You don't have to talk to us, but…"

"Alright, that's all I needed, thank you."

Emily turned back to her desk. Angelina looked to Matt, but he barely paused before putting his earphones back in. She should try and salvage the interview, shouldn't she?

She'd taken one step towards his desk, hand raised to nudge his shoulder, when Hobson thundered out of his meeting with Edward Lyne. He grabbed her by the shoulder and dragged her towards the exit. Thank God.

Making small attempts at waving to her new friends, she was soon pulled through the swing door, out to the corridor where they pressed the lift button. She almost opened her mouth, but Hobson shushed her with a single hiss. They stood like that until their exit arrived.

As the lift door closed, Hobson cut in before Angelina could say anything.

"I've no idea if Lyne did it. Okay?"

"Okay. I think Matt might've done it."

"Any reason?"

"He's pretty quiet."

"Right."

FOUR
EVENING PLANS

It was nearly eight as they weaved their way to the tube station in East London's trendy Dalston area. Angelina tried small talk about the case, but Hobson was preoccupied with reaching the underground as fast as possible. Probably worried about catching *Hipster* if he breathed too much of their air.

She imagined Hobson, the middle-aged dull-suited giant, in skinny jeans and huge glasses, and stifled a giggle. Not that she needed to hide it; he was striding too far ahead to notice.

She staggered over a tiny bicycle chained to a lamppost, hooking her foot through the spokes and stumbling forward. As she tottered like a giraffe, the bike itself scraped and rattled around the pavement. She yelled out, not using any real obscenities, but Hobson still looked round.

"Choi. Watch where you're going, you might damage that child's bike."

"It's not…" Despite the soreness in her arches, she laughed again. "It's not a *child's bike*, it's a BMX."

"Ah, I see," Hobson said. "I punched a cyclist once, he came clear off and hit the ground, but the bike kept going and took out the other guy I was chasing."

Angelina kept smiling despite her pain. "That sounds amazing."

"It was a better time, Choi. That shitty bike would never knock over a grown man."

In the end, Hobson dropped his pace and walked alongside Angelina. Nearby men in cardigans stopped laughing at her, probably out of fear Hobson would knock them off their bikes too.

"So, Choi," he said, "good news: Social Awesome are going to pay us to keep investigating this case."

"Wow. That was what the Lyne guy wanted to talk about?"

"Yeah."

She rolled the idea around her mind, as they approached the tube.

"Wow," she murmured again. "Not sure how I feel about that."

"Sadly, that was more or less my reaction."

They stopped outside the underground and stood awkwardly, as if on an age-inappropriate first date.

"So, get on the train and go home." He pointed into the station. "The bullshit continues at nine o'clock sharp tomorrow."

"Okay then." Angelina swung most of the way round on her ankle, before looking back at him. "Aren't you getting the tube back to South London too?"

"If only."

"You're going to break into that other house where the dog came from, aren't you?"

"Yes."

"Can I come?"

"Definitely not."

Angelina almost protested, but reined herself in. Other, shitter teenagers might have complained, but she was sensible enough to pick her battles.

So she nodded at him and entered the station to zip back south. It wasn't all bad news: with her flappy purple outfit and without the bloke cosplaying a gravedigger, she fitted right in on the escalator down to this particular tube stop.

Markham Road at night, only a few hours since Hobson was last here, felt quiet. The paparazzi were missing, evidently this double murder wasn't juicy enough. After all, the victims were a single guy in a studenty house share and some loser next door who *kept himself to himself.*

No, to get the presses printing, they'd need a dead kid, or at least a mutilated pretty woman. All that police tape around the two doorsteps was dropping off and sliding away.

For a moment, Hobson considered smashing his way into the other victim's home. But that would be stupid at the best of times, and he was meant to be avoiding senseless violence. He bought this uncharacteristically expensive black suit to encourage himself not to get covered in dust and blood.

The target house was mid-terrace, joined to others on both sides, and the garden backed on to other people's property. He could only think of one solution: turning back to the next residence, Hobson pounded on the door.

Ric McCabe answered quickly but with less obnoxious glee than before. He'd also dyed his hair from bright fire engine red to black. Did he think mournful hair would remove him from suspicion?

"Hello, um, Mister Hobson." McCabe waved. "How can I help you this time?"

"Evening, McCabe." He pointed over McCabe's shoulder. "Won't take up much of your time, just need to use the garden."

"What for?" McCabe said, laughing in advance of his own joke. "Are you going to do a reconstruction? Did you bring a puppy and a whip?"

"Just routine stuff." Hobson stared. "Nothing to worry about."

Standard trick: make him feel like he's the one being difficult. McCabe was a weakling, so Hobson got through to the garden in minutes. The guy tried to linger, but another look put an end to that.

For the second time that day, he peered at the dog track in front of him, fading as time passed. It was dark now, so he pulled out his torch to check his path through the tall grass to where the dog had entered. Once he reached the end, Hobson wrenched the fence slats aside and shoved his way through the jagged hole to the next garden over. It took effort to get his entire frame past the gap, Hobson being several times larger than a big wolfy dog, but in the end, he made it. The space only doubled in size, no-one would notice.

Whereas Pete and Ric's garden was a mess through neglect, the dog-owner's house hit the other end of the spectrum: beaten to death with over-use. Wheelbarrows full of rotten vegetables, metal pieces of engine, the stench of rust and a back door, hanging open.

Damn police, Hobson thought, they never clean up after themselves. Any moron could dash in there to destroy evidence, stash something, steal this bloke's stuff, whatever they wanted. And hadn't McCabe said there'd been no way for the dog to get out of the house?

He glanced again at the rubbish on the dead ground, including a pile of plastic sheeting knocked over, probably when the dog bolted. The fence looked even more rotten and brittle on this side, it wasn't hard to see how the hound made it through. He inspected it with the torch beam for a few seconds, and then turned to go inside.

The back door opened into the kitchen. All these terraced places used the same blueprint. But the sheer level of mess was off the scale – Hobson thought McCabe's unwashed dishes were bad, but this was rotting, disgusting, like everything had died. No wonder that dog had gone nuts – he was close to savaging someone himself.

There might've been a scattering of blood around too, but nothing was visible beneath the scum. Hobson would've held his nose, but he needed a hand free to open the next closed door, and the other one was busy with the torch. Knowing his luck, the police had missed a few bits of victim, and he was standing in chunks of brains.

Worst of all: he heard footsteps. Hobson froze and glanced back at the door to the garden. The noise was coming from inside the house, padding down the stairs and towards the living room – he assumed it was a living room behind this door, based on the layout of Pete and Ric's place.

Glancing behind him, he put down the torch and grabbed the most sturdy looking frying pan in sight, ignoring the mess of brown goo slopping out of it onto the floor. At least it missed his suit and polished boots.

Armed and ready, Hobson seized the living room door handle, pushed and threw it open. The light was already on inside; his fellow intruder was standing in front of the sofa, among a mess of takeaway cartons and empty dog food tins. To his utter relief and extreme disappointment, it was somebody he already knew.

Angelina slipped the key into the lock, twisting gently in the hope of not being noticed, or at least getting credit for *trying* not to make a noise. Unfortunately, when she pressed inwards on the massive wooden slab, it moved only a fraction before jarring.

The door latched into place with a stupid metal bar. She slapped it, hoping for a miracle, but no such luck. Not only did it barely move, but the noise got the attention of her mother. Well, *adoptive* mother.

"Angelina," she hurried towards the door, "it's a bit late isn't it? After ten?"

"Yes."

Her Mum pushed the door back into her face to disengage the bar. Once it moved back open, Angelina gazed into the bleak cushioning of home. Everything was beige and well-positioned – she'd almost rather live in the student houseshare hell of Ric and Pete.

"So," her Mum said before Angelina even put her bag down, "how was your first day? Did you catch any criminals?"

"Well, *actually*," Angelina said, "we're investigating a murder."

Her Mum's smile was small and patronising before, and now it ebbed away to nothing. "Which murder? Not the one on TV with the dogs?"

Angelina's heart sank. Her Mum was *such* a small-minded suburban white English person.

"Mum, come on, it's fine, Mister Hobson is with me the whole time and he's *massive*. No-one's going to hurt me."

"Oh, well," she said, "can he fight off a rabid wolf?"

"We discussed that this morning!"

Her mother sighed and marched off back to the kitchen. Angelina followed, pleased to see the oven firing up for a late dinner. At least she wouldn't have to cook for herself.

"So, you're doing paperwork while your boss investigates the murder?" she said.

"Well, I met a few people too, you know, it's important I learn, I thought we agreed I was doing this because it might be interesting for my psychology course…"

"No, Angelina, *you* said that, I told you it was silly, and then you went ahead anyway."

"I…"

"Is this what you want to do, Miss Choi?"

"Well, yes Mum." She nodded. "I'll stay out of danger, I promise. You know, I'm sure Mister Hobson has researched what I'm legally allowed to do."

Maybe. You never know.

"I don't want to see you on the news… running away from explosions or something, Angelina. Remember, you're only sixteen, some of these people might be dangerous."

"Right. No running. Got it. Can I watch TV with Dad while I eat?"

Angelina's mother sighed again, glanced at her daughter, then went to the freezer to get some fish.

She was unmistakable to Hobson even in mostly-darkness: straight hair, black coat, that oh-so-tired expression. Grabbing the torch from the kitchen with his free hand, he took the first step inside the living room, still uselessly holding a frying pan.

"Hello, Ellie," he said, trying not to sound like he ever panicked. She got her hand all the way inside her coat before identifying him.

She let it drop to her side, nice and casual. "John. I heard you were on this case. Surprised you haven't called."

"Yeah, I was getting to it."

"Worried I wouldn't pick up?" she said, with a small smile.

"Worried you wouldn't be helpful." Hobson strode into the room, kicking a few McDonald's bags aside and trying not to hold his nose, in case it made him look weak. He tossed the frying pan onto an armchair, and stepped away as it sent up a cloud of noxious-looking mess.

The dog food cans were everywhere, furniture clawed a thousand times, that table had a leg missing. There was a coil of turd poking through the upholstery and you couldn't sit on the sofa without worrying about falling into it. The inside of both doors was scratched into sawdust.

"Y'know, Ellie, I think they may have kept a dog in here," Hobson said, kicking the stained water bowl in the middle of the room.

"Wow. Thank God you came to point that out."

"Yeah," Hobson said, "anything good upstairs?"

"Considering I'm the police and you're not, John," she was looking at him, rather than the evidence, "I could easily tell you to fuck off out of my crime scene."

"I know," Hobson murmured, glancing behind the sofa cushions anyway and recoiling from the poo. "But I was hoping you'd let me off for old times' sake."

"I guessed. Are you really doing this case for Twitter followers? Because that's what I heard, and it's tacky."

"Is it? Shit. I rely on my intern to tell me what's tacky on the internet, Ellie, and she told me this was what all the detectives do nowadays."

"There's not going to be anything small and valuable down the back of the sofa if they kept the dog in here, John," she said as he yanked the cushions up from the base. "They couldn't risk it being found and eaten."

"Hey, Ellie, what if the dog wolfed down some crack before it mauled those two people?"

For a moment, there was almost a laugh, as he dropped the upholstery back into place, but happiness seemed the last straw for her. She backed him into the corner, towards the door he'd come through.

"John, you usually cover cheating husbands and petty shit. Are you only taking this case because you wanted an excuse to see your lovely police ex-wife?"

"Well, as a matter of fact," he announced, "it ain't just about Twitter followers anymore, I have a client paying me to turn over this dogshit." Even though Edward Lyne was creepier than a Christmas party at a second hand car dealership. "So yup, this is a real case."

Ellie didn't say anything at first, just stared. Tapped her pocket, as if considering seizing her handcuffs and arresting him, but it passed. In the end, she nodded and pointed towards the back door he'd entered through.

"Fuck off out of my crime scene, John."

"Can't I at least see if there's anything upstairs?"

"No."

"Or go out through the front door?"

"No."

"Bloody hell. You left the back door open, by the way."

FIVE
BAD BREAKFAST

Angelina wound her way past a man in a fancy dress pimp costume – surely no *real* pimp would wear that bright red velvet suit and enormous matching top hat? Taking her eyes off him, she looked around at the brown buildings, rubbish bags on the street and tiny indie supermarkets selling odd vegetables instead. She didn't normally come to this bit of South London, the part between her Kentish suburb and the centre, and it made her nervous.

She'd eased off the impressive clothes combinations for her second day, opting for a subdued black-and-blue ensemble to avoid drawing attention. Still got a few looks though.

Hoping someone would let her in quick, she knocked on the glass door to the Brightman Business Centre – an ambitious name for a two-storey crumbling maze of small rooms. Let's face facts, it was no Inspiration Gestation Station. Still, Peckham was taking off as a trendy area. There were cool-looking design firms in there, but also scary, shuffling guys who glared at her, wearing faded double-denim and exchanging suspicious parcels.

Through the door, she could see pretty receptionist Will, feet up on the desk and reading a magazine, hair just the right amount of askew even when he thought no-one was looking. Angelina assumed he'd be perusing some hip journal, but no, it was *Cameras & Photography Magazine*. Of course, she thought: Will was a real enthusiast, not some poser.

However, would be nice if he opened the door before the pimp caught up and tried to recruit her. Angelina didn't know what the small Asian girl fetish market was like in Peckham, but was in no hurry to find out. She banged on the glass harder, and Will finally looked up, nodded cheerily and swung upright.

He cruised across the reception area, didn't take long as it was a corridor with a small desk stuffed in, and pressed the button to let her in. His unironed dark shirt and thin red t-shirt clashed beautifully, topped off with a sweeping dyed-black fringe.

"Thanks," she smiled and mumbled.

"No problem," he said, squeezing back behind his desk, "but get Hobson to give you a card for the door. You don't wanna be stuck outside if you catch me on a toilet break."

"That's, um, good advice, thanks." She smiled, and thought with a sigh that this was one disadvantage of dressing down. She didn't feel good in herself wearing plain black trousers and a blouse, even if it was a blue one she liked. She had a hoodie over it for extra deflection.

There wasn't much corridor left before the stairs, so she took a few steps, before turning around, pretending she'd just remembered something. "Oh, by the way, you have the same name as the dead guy."

Will looked up from his camera magazine, still not seeming annoyed yet. "The one ripped apart by the dog?"

Angelina nodded, and he sighed. "I know, it was in all the papers. Always a shame to see a fellow William get shredded."

He paused, taking a moment's silence for his namesake, before looking back down. Angelina stung with disappointment – she'd thought of this conversation starter going to bed last night, and expected more from it.

Determined to try harder, she pushed through the doors and made for the stairs. The lack of a lift felt like a let-down, even though the building only had two floors.

Angelina reached Hobson's door and raised her hand to knock, before taking a breath and telling herself: this is your office now, you have as much right to walk in as he does. Please *please* don't let him be touching himself or anything.

She pushed the door aside and entered, finding Hobson sitting at his desk tapping irritably at his computer keyboard. No untoward behaviour of any kind. As she stepped over the threshold, he looked up and nodded.

"Morning Hobson."

"Choi," he said, sounding pleased to see her. If only Will had done the same. "Ready to get to work?"

"Yeah, in a sec," she said. "You know there's a guy hanging around here in a red velvet pimp suit? Complete with hat?"

"Oh, you mean The Pimp?"

"That's what you call him?"

Hobson shrugged. "Seemed to make sense."

"So he's really a pimp?"

"No idea."

"Shouldn't you want to know, as a detective?"

"Pay me a few hundred," Hobson said, with a chuckle. "I'll find out for you."

"Right."

She was about to turn on her computer and check the Twitter account, when Hobson stood up. "No rest today, Choi. Now we have a client instead of just the stupid internet, we're going to act like professionals."

Angelina liked the sound of this. "So what first?"

"The other victim, Pete Vole's next door neighbour who *owned* the dog," Hobson said, holding up a newspaper. It displayed a half-page Facebook-stolen picture of an angry looking shaven-headed man in a vest, accompanied by a mildly racist headline. Hobson pointed at his face as he declared the name: "Yalin Makozmo. They call him 'Yam' on the streets, according to this shitty journalism right here."

This was someone Angelina would cross the street to avoid. Possibly hide in a skip too. Did this make her racist? She wasn't white, she told herself, so that meant she couldn't be. "So, um," she stumbled over herself trying to sound calm, "we're going to look him up online?"

"Don't be stupid, Choi. The internet is for losers and paedophiles according to my newspaper. We're hitting some of his hangouts and getting the *real* story."

"Oh." Choi felt her enthusiasm from ten minutes ago leaking out through her boring Day Two black shoes, replaced by a rising tide of fear. "Great. My Mum will be so happy."

"Hello, Tony?"

"John Hobson? Is that you?"

"Yes. Listen, Tony…"

"Is it true you've hired a tiny Asian girl as your new partner?"

"She's not my partner, she's an intern."

"Since when do you have interns?"

"Since I ran out of money to pay people."

"Not just because of your whole self-punishment thing?"

"Not really in the mood for this, Tony. Got a question for you."

"Go on then."

"If I wanted to bet on a dogfight in North-East London, where would I go?"

"Since when do you bet on dogfights? Is this how you relax now instead of hitting people?"

"Maybe. Where would I go?"

"Lefty's, I s'pose."

"They have dogfights at Lefty's? I thought it was one of them McHellerman chain pubs? All cheap and bright?"

"It is, but it's gone bad, man."

"How does a Hellers pub go bad?"

"Don't go there, John. Trust me on this."

"Alright, well, thanks for your time."

Hobson dropped the phone before Tony could say anything else. Choi was already peering, as if she might ask questions about what she'd overheard.

So he headed her off at the pass. "Okay Choi, we're going to a Hellers pub. You're under the legal drinking age, so you'll fit in better than me."

She nodded and leapt to attention. "What's a '*Hellers pub*'? Like with pictures of the Devil?"

"Very funny." He pulled his coat off the back of the chair.

"No, seriously."

"It's a cheap chain of bars, serving microwave food and full of old men or teenagers." He stopped mid-movement to give her a critical stare. "You're sixteen, I thought you'd live there."

"Sorry," she said, seeming regretful. "Don't really go out drinking."

"Bloody hell." Hobson straightened and whipped the coat around his shoulders. "Well, you won't be starting today. Move it."

Angelina and Hobson came out of the same tube entrance as yesterday, but turned in the opposite direction, away from Markham Road. They'd estimated that The Left Hand – aka Lefty's – was only fifteen minutes walk from the scene of the wolf-murders, so definitely a place of interest.

They passed a row of shops, degrading from huge supermarkets to dingy holes as they moved away from the station, with their own crew of locals who never left. Hobson kept his eyes forward and stomped, making the occasional scathing comment. The laundrette covered in a thick layer of dust was heavily critiqued.

They reached a dark green-and-red building, a hanging sign proclaiming *The Left Hand* and displaying the dulled golden outline of a fist. Hobson gave the facade an eyeball, as if trying to establish dominance already.

Angelina just squinted. "Is this it?"

"Yeah. Looks the same as usual."

The deceptively light wooden doors flapped in the wind, and she peered through. Tables dropped at random across muddy-green carpet, manned by grey men in huge coats staring at their pints.

"Um, what do we do when we get in there?"

"Order a drink. No alcohol. Try not to look so fucking terrified."

"Thanks." Didn't stop her leg from shaking.

Hobson gave the pub another stern look, before pushing himself towards the entrance; Angelina slipped in behind him. The warmth enveloped her as she stood on a huge red welcome mat, feeling the atmosphere settle. Everything was dark and made of shiny wood.

The nearest decrepit man swung his eyes up at her over his massive beard, nodded, looked down again. A moment later, the next one along did the same. A woman and her husband glanced up from the crossword, continued the Mexican Nod, passing it along to the barman fiddling with the coffee machine.

Dirty plates slipped over each other on the tables, and it was only eleven in the morning. She followed Hobson up the room, wanting reassurance, but he wasn't paying attention.

Once they were standing at the bar, her feet sticking to patches of hard grey flooring, he leaned in to address the barman. He was tall and skinny, with a pointy nose, goatee beard and visible disdain. "Hi, two coffees and two breakfasts for me and my friend."

The lanky barman gave her a glance, as if considering what *friend* might be a euphemism for, before turning away to tap at his cash register. "And where are you sitting?"

"Over there." Hobson indicated the blackness at the back of the cavernous room. If the smattering of islandesque tables at the front had been weird, this was downright eerie. The layout over there was longer, thinner, darker, with booths embedded in the walls and awful lighting. No windows, no other customers. Not to mention, Angelina didn't even like coffee.

"What table number would that be, sir?"

"Who cares? There's no-one else there."

The barman looked like he might argue, before he met Hobson's eyes and went back to typing. "Yes, sir. That'll be nine twenty."

Hobson thrust a ten pound note at him, grabbed the change, then they meandered up to the back, among the maze of vacant tables.

Customers clustered at the front, scraping their plates and talking loudly in accents and languages she strained to understand. Many stared up towards Angelina and Hobson – by stepping into this grim back area, they'd sent some kind of message.

"So, um…" She eyeballed the empty seats all around, "where do you want to sit?"

"Booth over there."

So they did, plonking opposite each other. Hobson concentrated on glaring down everyone else, while Angelina tried to think of something to say. "So," she managed in the end, "where are all these teenagers?"

"At school, obviously. I'm not here so you can make friends, and you wouldn't like them anyway."

"So why *are* we here?"

"Curiosity, to be honest," he said. "I've been in a few crooked bars, but never a crooked McHellermans."

"And how is it?"

"Not sure. Everyone in here is either a criminal or a territorial alcoholic."

A short man in a leather jacket strode into the bar and sat straight down at a table near the door, entering into intense conversation with whoever was there already. Angelina tried not to look over, but Hobson just chortled.

"Well, they're definitely passing drugs under the table. This is fuckin' downmarket."

Across from their booth, the kitchen doors flapped and a man in white strode out. He wielded two plates, plonking them down in front of Hobson and Angelina before they could even look round at him.

The fried breakfast already looked dry and worn out, yet still warm to the touch, oozing its outline into the brown-white plate. Angelina peered, trying to work out which parts were safe to eat, while Hobson ignored it and looked up at the man who'd served them.

He was large, not a giant like Hobson but vastly overweight, seemingly held together by a greasy apron straining at all its knots. He didn't look happy. "You snotty pricks," he greeted them, "what do you mean *downmarket*?"

Hobson and Angelina exchanged glances. "Hi."

"Who the hell are you?"

Hobson grinned. The excitement of not being recognised must've shot straight to his head. "John Hobson. Do you have five minutes to talk?"

Angelina started to feel sick. Never visiting a McHellermans before had been a great decision. And that was before the fat guy shoved his way into their booth, prodding her up against the wall with his beefy arms and sliding the food towards her. She held her breath to avoid vomiting from the smell and hoped Hobson didn't have a long conversation planned.

This was a serious chat about a real murder, but nonetheless, Hobson stifled a grin. After all, his intern was squashed into a small space at the end of her bench-like seat by a morbidly obese chef. You had to laugh.

Trying to stay dour, he looked at his fry-up, wondering how many of these the chef must have eaten, and sliced into a veiny sausage. A thick trickle of yellowing fat ran out around the sides of his plate, and Hobson groaned. He was big enough to carry some extra weight, but there were limits.

He sopped the slice of meat around the beans to pick up some flavour, swallowed in one quick gulp, then looked back up. The chef didn't seem placated by Hobson's willingness to eat one forkful. Oh God, would he have to ingest this entire meal? Including that mushroom with thin crystal deposits on the skin?

"So what do you *want,* Mister Hobson?" The chef leaned forward, releasing the pressure on Choi's lungs a fraction. "Since this place is so beneath you."

"I wanted to ask you about the dog fights," Hobson said, trying to project confidence. "Do you have dog fights here?"

"Are you with the filth?"

"Nope."

Hobson knew it'd take a whole rasher of bacon to get over this hurdle. He stabbed his fork into it, managing not to wince as the solid pink block snapped open and splintered grey-black shards. It tasted as bad as it looked, crunching into a spiked blob in his mouth, but at least he didn't break any teeth.

The chef leaned in, showing Hobson was over the first hurdle, even as he growled: "I'll fuck you up if you're lying, okay?"

Hobson nodded, and went for another nugget of beans to absorb the remaining bacon. "And I'll be delighted to let you. What did you say your name was, sir?"

"They call me Micro." He leaned back, crushing the blood vessels in Choi's legs. She grimaced but Hobson stayed polite. Whenever a blowhard self-styled crime guy says *'They call me'* anything, it means they call themselves that, then beat the shit out of anyone who won't.

"Nice to meet you, Micro."

There was a tomato at the edge of the plate with a crusty outer layer, dribbling red bile thicker than ketchup – it looked like an animal's heart. He dug into the wooden bacon instead, hoping to avoid the tough redness. But as the next segment of pink splintering gristle went into his mouth, he coughed up a blob of rancid phlegm anyway.

His next Subway would taste like a fucking salad after this.

"So," Micro said, pleased by his efforts, "you wanted to know about the dog fights?"

"They do happen?"

"Anything small-time is fine by me, Mister Hobson. Little drug exchange here, small dogfight there. As long as you aren't serial killing or doing big time mafia shit, there's a home for you at Lefty's."

"For a generous cut, I suppose."

"Gotta make a living."

One last chance to build good will before the big questions. Hobson slashed into the decomposing mushroom and put the first chunk into his mouth. Surprisingly, it didn't crunch or crack, but dissolved into stodgy slime, tasting like soil and liquefied polystyrene. Hobson's stomach roared in disapproval. He'd known things would be rough when he swore to stop beating people for information, but he hadn't expected *this*.

Nonetheless, here goes nothing: "Did you know Yalin Makozmo, Micro?"

"The dead guy? Yeah, what a fuck-up *that* was. Eaten by his own dog. Shame though," Micro shook his head, vibrating Choi's entire body, "they were good animals. Yam's dogs never lost. He made almost as much from those fights as I did."

"Hm." Hobson kept his cool, whereas Choi peered at Micro wide-eyed, despite her obvious discomfort. To keep things rolling, he ate another shard of sausage and didn't retch any back up.

"So he was good, then? Or his dogs were?"

"Christ, yes. Savage fuckin' beasts, Mister Hobson. Honestly, not *that* surprised what happened to him – he must've done some dark shit to get the bastards so rabid."

"Right. And Yam never mentioned his neighbours to you at all?"

"The *other* dead guy?" Micro said.

"Yes."

There was a pause. Micro sat back and surveyed the table. An excited Choi leaned in so far, Hobson was amazed the big bastard didn't feel squashed.

"He might've mentioned them. What's it worth?" Micro said.

Giving the remains of his breakfast a sad, slow look, Hobson knew there was only one thing to do. Trying not to think too hard, he plunged his fork into the centre of that crusty tomato and ate the whole thing in one go.

In the end, it didn't taste like anyone's internal organs – more a small tennis ball filled with paper, dusty ball bearings and rotten ketchup. He chewed through it, feeling the innards scrape on his teeth and plunge, sour and full of bits, onto his taste buds. A burst of blackened, cancerous mess flooded up and down his nose and throat. He washed it down with a mouthful of coffee, not as rancid as the meal, and met Micro's eyes again.

The chef took a long expectant pause, probably seeing if that tomato would come back. Hobson gulped, and everything stayed down. Just.

Micro burst out laughing. "Okay, then. Yam liked his neighbours, as far as I knew."

"Really?"

"Yes. Never said a bad word about them, one time I went round to drop off some cash, and he was chatting to the dead one over the fence."

"So the dog torturers and Twitter morons were all best friends?"

"That's how it looks. I mean, Yam and I weren't close, but can't see any reason he'd up and kill one of them. They weren't into anything dirty, far as I know."

Hobson tapped the table, Choi looked just as bemused. Before he could think of any more questions, there was a commotion at the front of the pub as a small crowd in cheap suits shoved their way in.

"Well," Micro rose from the booth, causing a small tremor, "that's the lunchtime rush, I'd best be on my way. Nice meeting you, Mister Hobson, and if you come again, I might even make you a proper breakfast."

For a flash of a moment, Hobson wanted to punch Micro in the face, but let the need wash over him. Tried a few deep breaths, which only brought the taste of stomach juice back. By the time he'd choked that back, Micro was gone.

Choi cut off a slice of her bacon, which didn't snap like a twig, and chewed for a short while.

"Actually, Hobson, this is pretty good," she said, with a gleeful smile.

"Great." He let his head slip into his hands.

"So what now?"

"Well, Choi, in a moment, we head back to Social Awesome and check in with the client." He forced himself up to his feet, insides swaying.

"But first?" she said.

"First, I'm going to visit Mister Micro's toilets and stick my fingers right down my throat. But enjoy your breakfast while I'm gone."

"Right."

She dropped her cutlery with a satisfying clatter as he left the booth.

SIX
WITNESSES

On their way to the Inspiration Gestation Station to check in with Edward Lyne, Hobson and Choi swung into a nearby branch of production line lunch shop Subway. He'd not been able to get them out of his head since that awful breakfast.

"Second day running?" Choi murmured. "Wow, you really like your subs."

"I don't *really* like them," Hobson said, "I just fancied one after that manky fry-up."

"That's how they get you, y'know? First a mild inclination, then a desperate need."

"I'll be fine, Choi."

They joined the queue, standing in silence while Choi checked her phone. Only a day ago, Hobson thought, she was too scared of upsetting the new boss to ignore him in favour of Twitter.

Before he could complain, the intern saw something over the top of her phone and nudged him. "Hobson! Look! It's Social Awesome!"

Sure enough, it was a group of them: receptionist

Lettie Vole, her brother Pete, quiet programmer Matt (who Choi believed was a heartless killer), and Jacq, front desk woman of the whole Inspiration Defecation Installation. Hobson wasn't so much impressed by Choi noticing them as annoyed with himself for not doing so – wasn't he meant to be a detective?

After all, they were hardly hiding, just slumped around a small table eating sandwiches. Maybe they'd faded out of view because they were *using* the tables provided in Subway – who would risk food on those crusty plastic spindles?

Of course, the moment Hobson and Choi noticed the Social Awesome crew, they all looked up and around. Only for a moment, though – after a short, unified stare, the whole table went back to their food, talking quieter than before.

Hobson went back to reading the menu, but out of the corner of his eye, noticed Choi giving them a tiny, awkward wave.

It was the kind of twee hand-flutter Hobson hated, but it seemed to strike a chord with these bastards. They smiled and waved back – except sullen potential psychopath Matt, who kept examining the swirling table pattern.

"Choi," he hissed, a plan forming, "do you think you can get *in* with these people?"

"Who?"

"That lot," he muttered, taking care not to gesticulate, "the Social Awesome awful cool Twitter nightmare over there. They seem to respond to whatever it is you do with your arms and your dithering."

"My arms?"

"Look," he said, "get your sandwich, then go over there and make friends. I'll cut my losses and go ahead to their office."

"Wow." Choi's eyes widened, as if he'd asked her to scale a tall building. "Do you think I could prove Matt killed William?"

Hobson only sighed. "Maybe focus on being friendly. Ask them why they Twitter, or something."

She sighed right back at him. "Okay."

"Okay."

Angelina walked over to their table, putting one foot in front of the other. She decided to open her attack with another small wave. After all, the last one had gone pretty well – this time, though, they seemed bewildered.

"Hello," she added, standing next to their lunch table and gazing. What if she couldn't get them to accept her? Would she have to go and eat lunch on her own? It'd be like school. Lettie moved to assume her role as grumpy gatekeeper, even though she wasn't behind a reception desk, but a friendlier face leapt in first.

"Hi Miss Choi!" Jacq sounded so overjoyed to see her again, Angelina found it a little annoying. "Are you just having some lunch?"

"Um, yeah. You?"

This time, angry Lettie got straight in there. "What do you think, Miss Detective? We're in a sandwich shop, eating sandwiches, at lunchtime. What can you deduce from this?"

"Oh, well, I'm only an intern, but I thought you might be here for work – you know, just so you can tweet and Instagram and stuff about it." Nervous laugh. "Sound like you're doing something cool."

To her relief, everyone laughed, although Lettie's was more a scathing cackle.

"Oh, Angelina, this isn't us being cool," Pete leapt in, "this is merely lunch. Subway isn't cool anymore."

"Right, of course." She smiled again, and Pete and Lettie pulled their chairs apart to make space for her. She sat down before they could change their minds and shut the gap.

"So," she didn't want to lose momentum, "what *is* cool?"

"You can't label cool, sweetheart," Pete continued, "but it's a good bet that if the place is owned by an international corporation, it ain't."

Over Pete's shoulder, Angelina caught Lettie grimacing at her brother's smugness, as Jacq burst out laughing.

"Yeah," Lettie snorted, "you're so awesome, Pete, you're a tastemaker – if that taste was bile and cruddy Subway bread. So, Miss Detective," she continued over Pete's look, "found out whodunnit yet?"

Angelina's eyes widened, as she became very interested in unpicking the paper around her sandwich. "Well, y'know, we're looking into it."

Right then, mid-sentence, she had an amazing idea: "Who do *you guys* think did it?"

She tried not to stare at Matt. He hadn't spoken since she sat down, which struck her as suspicious.

"You want us to do your job for you?" Lettie smirked.

"I don't get paid," she said. "Don't you want to find out who killed your colleague?"

"Ha." Lettie thought for a moment, before coming back with: "I think it was our boss. Got sick of everyone hating William instead of working."

"Nah," Pete grinned and leapt in, "It's gotta be Jacq. She's just too nice to be true."

Everyone looked over at the accused, who blushed, before mumbling: "Well, I don't know who it was. Maybe the dog got in by itself?"

"What," Pete laughed, "smashed through our lock with a doggy crowbar?"

They all rewarded that with a chuckle except Angelina, who turned towards the one person who still hadn't spoken. "Who do *you* think it was, Matt?"

The final member of the party was staring hard at his sandwich from under his own fringe. He took a bite, before glancing up to acknowledge his name.

"Dunno," he said at last, "maybe Jacq's right about the dog. Did you guys see this tweet about cows that's going round?"

The whole table turned towards their phones, even Angelina, but she kept one eye on Matt.

Security at the Inspiration Gestation Station was a joke, Hobson thought. That's the problem with these way-too-trendy places: too busy looking good, rather than locking out psychos. With regular receptionist Jacq off at lunch, some spotty under-eighteen was manning the desk.

Hobson strolled past him with a firm nod. The kid was far too scared to stop a determined older man in enormous coat and black suit. By the time the front door to the building shut behind him, Hobson was in the flowery lift heading up to the Social Awesome offices.

As the lift hummed, he caught the stink of lunches, and once again hungered for a sandwich.

Maybe Edward Lyne would supply a snack – he was the one who requested a check in, after all.

The lift doors slid open and Hobson exited into the strip lights and sparse, empty desks of Social Awesome's offices. One wall of the room was entirely windows, and right now, clouds spread across, throwing the whole place into shade. Only Emily was at her desk on the other side of the room, Lyne's side-office door closed.

Well, they'd not spoken to her yet. Hobson strolled over to Emily's corner. Her well-maintained blonde head looked up as he approached, placing a half-eaten sandwich back in her lunchbox. She kept it inside the cling film, apple pushed right up against one corner. Emily was well organised. Mind of a killer, Hobson thought, and then worried that was the kind of simplistic observation Choi would make.

"Miss Allen?" he said.

She held his eye for a moment, before looking back at her screen. "Afternoon, Mister Hobson."

"Everything alright?"

"Fine. You?"

"Yeah," Hobson sighed, "not bad."

From this close up, she was obviously beautiful – a well-kept, fragile prettiness he rarely encountered in his line of work, marred by her obvious annoyance. She took another glance, checking whether he'd gone yet.

Since he refused to take the hint, she forced out some small talk: "So, how's the investigation going?"

"It's fine, I think. Had to eat a pretty bad fry-up but that's just the job."

"Sounds like hard work you do," Emily said. He'd been making a joke, dammit. She gave him a withering look, then continued typing an email he couldn't quite read. Probably a string of abuse.

"So," he began, knowing this wouldn't end well, but since he was here, he might as well do his pitiful job. "Why didn't you go to lunch with the others?"

"What?"

"Choi and I saw the rest of 'em in Subway," Hobson said, air of triumph settling. "Why're you sitting at your desk instead of going along?"

"I don't really see how it's your business, Mister Hobson, but if you must know, I find Matt awkward company, so I'm enjoying not having to sit near him for a while." Emily straightened her spine into an insectoid defence position. His chances of getting a date pissed away with every word.

"Uh-huh. I thought you were good friends with thingy." He snapped his fingers. "Jacqueline from downstairs."

"Friends, yes, not her mum. She can look after herself." And, after a stare from Hobson: "Fine, sometimes she can't, but I see her plenty out of work."

"So Matt makes you uncomfortable because, what, he fancies you?"

"Yes! He asked me out and I said no! Happy?"

Hobson was grinning so wide, it was a hard charge to deny. Sex was definitely off the cards now, but he was so pleased to have *won* the conversation, he barely cared. "And this was before William died?"

"Yes! After I went on the date with William! I mean, he was quiet about it, but it was still awkward."

"Right."

Hobson tapped his foot. Before he came up with anything else, though, the lift started to roar again.

The rest of the gang were back, he could hear loud chatter drifting through the doors already. If he had to guess, Lettie Vole yelling at her brother.

The shrill noise echoed a moment longer, before the doors whirled open and everything burst right into the office. The buzz of four people talking among themselves mowed down the awkward silence between Hobson and Emily.

Well, most of them talking. Choi was over by reception chatting to the redhead siblings, Matt scuttled away from the group, heading back over towards that same corner to take his seat near Emily.

Well, Hobson thought, since he was here: "Hi Matt."

Matt mumbled something that might've been a hello and kept going, always looking at the floor.

"Right. Good lunch? Everything alright?"

"Yeah, thanks." Matt said, at least looking up. "Your assistant made us take some guesses at who killed William."

"Really?" He stared daggers at Choi with his mind, though not his eyes. "And who was it?"

"Um, we're not sure." He looked down at his computer. "Maybe you should talk to your friend."

Hobson glanced down at Emily, but even she seemed bewildered. So much so, she gazed at him with wide-eyed empathy, even though a minute earlier she was willing him to fuck off.

"Right. Thanks."

He nodded at the two of them, before going back over to Choi. He affected a stern, intimidating walk, loud enough to get Lettie and Pete looking over their shoulders. They scattered as he came nearer, knocking chairs aside as they went.

Once he arrived, he swept past Lettie's desk and took Choi aside. "So," he said, not bothering with pleasantries. "Matt said to talk to you."

"Oh, um, he passed me a note as we left Subway. He'd scribbled it on his sandwich wrapper."

"Saying what? *I killed William, I'm so sorry*?"

"No."

"Damn."

"He, um, wants me, um, well, us I guess, to meet him here after work at seven this evening, he says he has some information."

"Can't he just text you the sodding information?"

"I think he's scared of something."

Hobson growled. "I'm pretty sure he's scared of everything."

"So are we going to do it?"

"Yeah."

"Okay," Hobson nodded at the side-room. "Well, we're here, I'd better have this check-up with the boss."

Angelina gazed at it, hoping she was imagining the strange lights and weird sounds within. "Will you be okay in there?"

"Choi, he's got the muscle definition of a dead kitten, I'll be fine."

The rest of Social Awesome were working. Even Lettie and Pete left each other alone for the moment, staring at their monitors and sometimes muttering. Angelina didn't yet have the intuition to know if something was wrong or they were just socially awkward. Emily didn't seem too geeky, for example. Now her head was starting to ache again, until Hobson slapped her on the shoulder.

"Okay Choi, I'm going in. Talk to them if you must, but try not to ruin everything."

With those words, he stamped over to Edward Lyne's office door, loud enough to get everyone looking over from their individual seats.

As he knocked and entered, they turned their attention to poor, tiny Angelina Choi standing at the entrance, alone in a huge empty space. She would've considered jumping down the lift shaft if the door had been open.

Instead, she waved childishly at the nearest desk – she could charm them like this a second time, couldn't she? Even when the recipient was as grumpy as Lettie Vole?

"Mister Hobson. How are you? Take a seat."

"Thanks, Mister Lyne. So, what did you want to talk about?"

"I just wondered how the investigation was going. Have you got everything under control?"

"No major progress since you asked me the same questions yesterday. My assistant and I are talking to some people."

"I thought she was your intern?"

"Depends."

"And these people, do they include my employees?"

"Yes. I'm afraid the victim was a nerd and didn't seem to have a life outside work."

"I'd rather Social Awesome wasn't involved."

"Mister Lyne, sorry if this wasn't clear, but when you took me on to look into this case, I didn't promise to leave your company out of it."

"I see."

"Would you *like* me to do that?"

"No, of course not."

"Good. So, while we're here, one question, if you don't mind."

"Which is?"

"Why *did* everyone hate William Lane?"

"Man, Angie," Lettie sighed, "your job sounds so much more fun than mine."

"Oh, I don't know," she replied, bristling only a little at being called *Angie.* "I mean, I do get to investigate a murder, but this morning I got squashed against the wall of a pub by a fat guy, and I've been yelled at, sent for sandwiches, seen blood dribbling from a corpse."

She smiled and kicked back in the spare chair near Lettie's desk.

It turned out, all she had to do was show interest in Lettie's job, and the bored woman was anyone's. Still, hard work pretending to care. Lettie answered phones, filled in expense forms, ordered stationary, argued with her brother all day – all so dull.

"Oh, and the other thing," Lettie lurched down her endless list of grievances, "bloody Pete hitting on every woman who walks through the door." She kept her voice low, as *bloody Pete* was only a few desks away. "I mean, maybe it's because he's my brother – I mean, *yick* – but it's not just that he hits on them, it's that he does it *so badly*. Don't touch him, Angie, no matter how much he begs."

Angelina felt herself turning a little pink. "He did call me *sweetheart* earlier, which I didn't like, but I just ignored him."

"Good. Keep doing that." Lettie said, shaking her head. "Punch him if you have to."

"Thanks, I'll keep that in mind." Determined to get the conversation away from sex, she flailed for a new question: "Um, what about William the dead guy? Did you like him?"

Lettie laughed. "You mean in a sex way?"

"I don't know what you mean, Mister Hobson. William was a good employee, always punctual, friendly. Maybe not outgoing and gregarious, but that's what we have Emily and Pete for. He sat back here with Matt, he only talked to clients by email."

"So he was popular? No housemate tensions with Pete? No awkwardness with Emily after their date? Everything was tickety-amazing?"

"Maybe not perfect, you know, we're all passionate people working in a creative field, there were disagreements, I'm not sure William always fitted in perfectly with how we wanted to do things."

"Uh-huh. Two things: you work in social media, it's about as creative as shitting up a bathroom wall. Secondly, I've spoken to your people, and they hate him. Why?"

"We've always done things a certain *way*, Mister Hobson. William didn't always like it."

"Why didn't you fire him, then?"

"I thought he might have something to contribute."

"Right."

"For whatever it's worth, Mister Hobson, I didn't kill him, and I'd appreciate it if you found whoever did."

"Even if it's one of your staff?"

"I suppose so."

"Do I have to come in for another check-in tomorrow?"

"Not unless you have something to report."

"Fantastic."

Once Angelina established, no, she definitely wasn't asking about William *in a sex way*, Lettie fell quiet. In fact, she insisted on going alone to get a cup of tea, although she offered to bring one back for Angelina. Did their budding friendship still stand a chance?

A desperate need for approval might not be a great attribute for undercover work, Angelina thought, as she checked her phone. A few people on Twitter were asking how the case was going – she'd check with Hobson first before replying.

She glimpsed Matt looking over at her, but he turned back to his monitor as soon as she met his eyes. That face couldn't look any more miserable.

"Here you go." A mug of tea clattered in front of her, and Angelina smiled. She wasn't a huge fan of hot caffeinated beverages, to tell the truth, but seemed rude to say no.

"Thanks."

Lettie sighed back down into her chair, and there was a silence.

"Okay, look," Lettie said, eyes wide and starting to go as red as her hair. "William was just earnest, in a quiet way. He was young, straight out of school, and he wanted to… *do* a bit more than other people."

"What do you mean?"

"I mean, y'know, look at us," she said, almost in a whisper. "We're hardly a machine. We do the bare minimum, we collect, we drink. It's fine. I mean, I'm not a high-ranking part of the company, but Will was so moany about everything we weren't doing, it even got on *my* nerves."

"So you think someone killed him for being annoying at the office?"

She shrugged. "I'm not sure. Seems a stupid reason to kill someone to me. But someone who had a lot to lose if the company folded?"

"Why would it fold?"

"Because someone might call all our clients and tell them how little we actually do?"

Angelina looked over at Edward Lyne's office, her own eyes growing as saucer-like as Lettie's. "Shit."

For a moment, she wondered if Hobson was in real danger. Should she charge Lyne's door? Would her weedy frame even survive a full-on ramming impact? If Hobson couldn't overpower him, what good would *she* do?

Before she dislocated her shoulder finding out, the target door flew open and Hobson stormed out yet again. Angelina, well trained in this exit move by now, nodded to Lettie. "Um, see you later?"

To her pleasure, she got a "Sure thing, Angie" back, just in time to peel away when Hobson came past. A few moments later, they were back in the lift.

"So," she began, "I'm a bit worried it might be Edward Lyne."

"Dammit Choi, I was finally starting to agree with you about it being Matt."

"Sorry."

"Never mind." Hobson grinned. "We'll come back in a few hours for this after hours meeting, he'll confess, then you'll really have earned the nothing I pay you.

SEVEN
COULD BE DARKER

They'd debated locations for evening food, but the winner was clear from the start: Subway, yet again – Hobson still wanted that sandwich. He got the full footlong meatball, whilst Choi sat there, moaning that she *couldn't* have the same thing for *both* major meals of the day.

The more she sulked, the slower Hobson ate.

After he took her down the road and bought her a Cornish pasty, they found themselves on a bench, a few feet back from the street near some grass and a church. She devoured the whole brown pastry-blob in less than a minute. For such a tiny thing, she ate like a wolf – maybe she was the killer. At last, both finished, they stared at the sky.

The Inspiration Gestation Station was only five minutes' walk away, and they tried to wait away from public transport. Didn't want any of the Social Awesome staff to pass by and realise they were heading back later.

"So, Choi," Hobson said, "what do you think Matt

wants to tell us? Now you've decided he's not the killer."

"Maybe he's gonna tell us the same thing Lettie told me – Lyne killed William to keep Social Awesome going."

"She didn't *really* tell you that, and Lyne told me he didn't do it."

"And he would never tell a lie? He's basically Skeletor," Choi said, grinning in satisfaction at her own insight.

"How does someone as young as you know who Skeletor is?"

"From the internet, other people mention it."

"Right. Good." Hobson sighed and brought the conversation back around. "There isn't some dark secret, y'know? They're just a bit lazy. You don't kill someone to stop that spreading, you just pay them off."

"But Lyne's evil," she said, as if he'd missed the winning argument.

"Real people aren't *evil*, Choi." Although, he must admit, Edward Lyne often seemed despicable. "So you've gone off Matt as a suspect?"

"Maybe he's just creepy."

"Maybe," he said, happier with that sentiment.

The dark settled, the commuters were drifting out onto the pavement around them. Most were on their way to the area's many bars and shops, ready for action after escaping the office. Their ties were steadily loosening. Hobson kept his pushed up tight. "When did Matt's stupid note say we should meet him?" he said, foot twitching.

"Seven."

Hobson looked at his watch. "Half an hour's time. Let's get this over with."

They got up, threw their rubbish away and joined the surge of people down the road, watching for the shadow of the IGS in the left darkness. The building's decor was less infuriating when he couldn't see it.

When Angelina first visited the Inspiration Gestation Station, it felt like a friendly, welcoming place. She enjoyed the chatty receptionist and bright colours. Social Awesome's business environment seemed way better than her own, at first anyway.

That hadn't lasted long. Not only were Social Awesome not all they seemed, but returning to the IGS late at night, the sunlight dissolved away, it didn't seem as wonderful. The sharp angles loomed above her like a haunted rock. All the lights were out, except Social Awesome's. Even the reception area was in darkness. She jumped out of her skin as a car started nearby, Hobson glared at her.

An intercom sat on the wall next to the glass card-locked front door, and she pointed at it, nervous. "Um, Matt's note said to buzz him and he'd come let us in."

"This really is stupid," Hobson said.

"He's a nervous guy, maybe he feels safe behind a locked door."

Hobson tutted, then took a closer look at the front door of the IGS – it was ajar. His body tensed up, fists flexing, and Angelina shrank even more.

He stretched out a foot and kicked the door. Giving no resistance, it drifted inwards. "Doesn't seem like we need the buzzer."

"Yeah," Angelina said, adding for the sake of it: "Guess he left it open for us."

"Yeah."

Angelina broke eye contact with Hobson. She mounted the small step from the pavement, ready to march inside.

Before a single cell of her body crossed the threshold, Hobson grabbed her by the shoulder and tugged her backwards. She gasped, so unprepared that her feet almost left the floor.

"Choi," he growled, "just in case it wasn't fucking clear, I will be first into the darkened building, okay?"

"Yeah, sure, no worries." His grip pinched into her and she tried to recoil. With so little flab on her shoulder, Hobson was squeezing the bone. Still, he waited a few moments, as if making sure she'd heard her own words, before letting go and dropping the weight back onto her feet.

"You don't need to pull me around," Angelina grumbled, "I'm not a little girl."

"Yes, you are."

"Why'd you let me come at all, then?"

Hobson looked up at the black windows, streetlight reflections floating in them like grim stars. "Right now, Choi, I'm not sure. But you're already here, and I'm not leaving you out on the street either."

Exchanging one last look, they tugged the door open and stepped into the glowing reception area. Nothing happened, no alarm went off. A few moments after they entered, a weak strip light shuddered into life on some kind of automatic sensor. Angelina breathed a sigh of relief, looking around and taking comfort in the silly pasture designs on the walls. The desk was tidy, door to the stairs closed and dark. No-one was there, nothing was wrong.

"Lift's dead," Hobson muttered.

"What?"

"The lift, they've turned it off. Reception closes at six according to the sign, guess Jacq shuts it down when she leaves."

"Right."

Shaking his head, Hobson went back over to the door, reached outside and pressed the *Social Awesome* button on the intercom. It rang, sounding more desperate to Angelina with every tone, until the machine gave up the ghost. Silence fell, and the cold was flooding through the open door now, chilling her even further.

"Brilliant," he said.

"Now what?" Angelina hoped the answer involved going home.

"We get the fuck out of here, Choi," he snapped.

"Thank God."

"And next time a nerd asks you out, I'm not chaperoning."

Before she could blush or complain, there was a scream, a yell, a clear human awful noise. It pierced through the walls of the building and almost squeezed the Cornish pasty out of Angelina's stomach. Finally, it ended with a thud. She yelled, jumped, landed, then spat out: *"HobsonWhatTheFuckWasThat?"*.

He glanced at the lift, and then behind him at the door marked *STAIRS*. "Don't know," he said, "but think it came from in there."

"Well, let's run away from it, then."

Hobson looked through the gloomy porthole in the door. "There's something dripping down in there."

"Let's *definitely* run away."

"Gimme a second."

Hobson poked the stairwell door open bit-by-bit, stepping inside once there was space. He took a wide diversion around something just the other side, underneath the staircase itself. The lights flickered on in the porthole as he entered, revealing him edging towards the back wall, before climbing the stairs slowly.

After another glance out to the street, Angelina crept up to the window in the door. There was something falling down in there, from the first floor to ground level. A steady rush of blood poured through the plastic railings and smashed into the floor. It was thickening and red, congealing around the edges of its own splat.

Gulping, she looked up, and saw the source: a ripped up torso of a body creeping towards the edge of the next level, glooping its insides everywhere. Hobson was kneeling down next to the remains, eyes wide and back of huge hand covering his mouth and nose.

Angelina pushed the door gently open – enough to let her voice through, without risking a trip into the thin waterfall of gore.

"Hobson?"

"Yeah."

"Is that Matt?"

He looked down towards her and nodded.

Angelina inhaled so deep, she almost made herself sick.

The door slammed downstairs, and Hobson sighed. Was it too late to send Choi out for a sandwich again?

Blood sopped through Matt's clothing, dripping between the claw-marks in his shirt and trousers. His left forearm was missing, right hand still clasped loose around the stump. The amputation and hacked-up side of his torso oozed the most red sludge. His neck and head, though, somehow escaped mauling. Whatever attacked him lacked high reach, and he'd stayed upright. For a while, at least.

The longer the body lay there, the more the mess pooled. His straggly hair lay in the blood puddles, sticking together and turning a dirty red-brown colour. The eyes were cold, face sad. This one wasn't the killer, Hobson concluded, and felt a little guilty that he and his assistant spent so long asking if he was. But, again, that was the job.

The dead smell was travelling up Hobson's nose and down his throat. He stood up again, taking a firm step back.

It looked like a dog had killed this one too. Could be the same animal that did William Lane, maybe a different beast, but the bite marks clinched it. Fucking hell. A canine serial killer?

Hobson looked beyond the body, to a trail of blood splurges stretching up the stairs. Matt stumbled from where he'd been attacked, down the building until he bled to a halt right here. If the original mauling site wasn't Social Awesome on the third floor, he'd ditch detective work right now – maybe go into online marketing.

He looked down at the door he'd come through. The lift was turned off, and this stairwell the only other way up. So the kid was safe in reception alone, surely? He texted her: *Choi, sit tight, going to check all clear up there. Text if anything happens.*

Breathing deep with anticipation, Hobson clenched his fists and started climbing the stairs.

Angelina wasn't sure if this was a good strategic position. She cowered behind the reception desk, staring at the crap underneath it: books, magazines, couple of dusty pairs of shoes, bin overflowing with tissues and crisp packets, wires and receipts leaking from the drawers. Jacq did not keep a tidy workplace.

All this filth hung around her head as she pressed further into the footwell. She liked being encased on all sides, away from the dripping corpse.

Should she go outside? Run away home? Follow Hobson upstairs?

Her phone pinged, and a text from Hobson popped up. *Sit tight,* he said? At least she had permission from her supervising adult to do nothing, but it still didn't feel right to her. As she read his text, Angelina realised – she had a mobile.

Feeling stupid for taking a few minutes to notice her beloved smartphone, she flicked to the telephone keypad and dialled. Waited a few seconds for someone to pick up, then said: "Yes, hi, police please? I've got a, um, corpse over here."

The blood never ran out, all the way to the third floor. It flowed softer as Hobson climbed, though. Matt's grip on his injuries must've weakened as he descended the stairs.

No sign of his severed forearm, nor a dog running along chewing it like a lucky bone. Every so often, the trail of half-shaded red footsteps thinned or thickened, as if Matt had swayed back and forth, but never fallen. Fair enough, Hobson could respect that.

Matthew Michaelson may have been a scrawny, maladjusted loser, but he'd fought to survive.

And failed, but nonetheless, credit where it was due.

Hobson reached the door to Social Awesome. The lights were still on. He stole a glance through the window into the office, trying not to be obvious.

No humans nor animals, not a single sound, but quite the fucking blood stain. Filmed over Lettie's desk at the front, all the way to Matt's own chair at the back. It was thin but obvious; the dark carpet shone with red highlights. The centrepiece of the whole awful tableau, of course, was Matt's forearm, white with red specks, flat in the middle of the stain. Horrible teeth marks in the wrist – the dog had seized it as a plaything after all.

Hobson pushed the door open gently and stepped inside, wincing as the carpet squelched underfoot. He'd been so careful to avoid standing in the blood until now.

Moving aside to escape the slime, he looked across the room. There were signs of a struggle, a few stains on computers, books strewn around, but this hadn't been an epic battle. The dog swiped into its victim until it was pulled away, leaving Matt alive to embark on a post-attack hike down the stairs. Why?

Squinting, as if that helped him see into the past, Hobson made his way towards Matt's desk at the back.

There was a crunch underfoot, shuddering up Hobson's leg. Oh good fuck, please don't be a tooth. When he looked down, though, it was a piece of plastic – one of many, strewn along the floor. A mobile phone stamped into fragments, probably by a human heel or handheld weapon. Crucially, didn't look like animal jaws had tried to bite it.

He took another look around the room, but nothing and no-one jumped out at him. Nearly time to call the cops and let Ellie have a go, see if her forensic chaps could turn up anything.

As Hobson went for the door again, there was a sudden mechanical hum, shaking out of the walls themselves. It took a second to realise it was the lift coming back to life, the lights above it flickering on. The glowing arrow indicating it was heading down from the second floor, towards the reception area where he'd left Choi.

Angelina sat against the front of the reception desk, playing with her phone and resisting the urge to livetweet this experience. Would get her *loads* of new followers. She eyeballed the stairwell again.

No sign of the police or Hobson. She considered calling him to check in, when the lift started up with a hiss. Fear leapt straight back up her neck to squeeze her brain tight. She looked at the indicators up top, and confirmed it was lowering towards her. Well, she figured, probably Hobson coming back down – the lazy old man figured out how to switch it on, so cut out the effort of walking down the stairs.

Yeah, that'd be it. But still, as the lift closed in on the reception floor, Angelina's feet were twitching, wanting to flee or leap back behind Jacq's desk.

The lift squeaked to a halt, and its flower-painted doors began to open. Angelina hoped that growl was her stomach.

Smashing his way down the stairs, sending an echo through the Inspiration Gestation Station with every jump, Hobson smeared blood everywhere. Ellie would be furious about this mess, absolutely enraged, but she could wait her turn. If the dog was hiding in the lift and ripped Choi to pieces while he was looking after her, he was *fucked*.

Not only had he left her alone to chase a fight, he hadn't even found anything useful.

Hobson leapt down from the second floor and put a stomp into his landing, trying to shake himself out of this funk. He smashed down, barely a foot from the gooey corpse of Matt. Pure luck he hadn't pulped one of the dead legs. As it was, Hobson's torso dipped to shock-absorb his landing, and he inhaled a gory stench that turned his stomach.

Standing back up, he slowed for a minute, clinging to the wall as he skirted around the body. At last, he resumed his headlong kamikaze dive down the remaining stairs.

His boots were so slippery with blood, his grip on the floor slid away during his last take-off. The landing still worked, although with definite stickiness when he pulled his feet up again.

Hobson wrenched the door at the bottom open and rushed out, ready to fight his wolf.

Angelina thought about running, but it seemed pointless. The lift doors were half open before she reached even that conclusion. As the nauseous shudder travelled up her throat and became a mouthful of retch, she realised the growling sound was her stomach rumbling after all.

Angelina stepped forward, shaking as a tumbling mane of brown curly hair and hippy knitwear stumbled forward out of the lift, tripping over its own feet. At last, it looked up at her and gasped. There was blood rolling off her forehead, staining her hair and sleeves. Seemed you weren't anybody tonight unless you were dripping with human fluid.

"Jacq!" Angelina hesitated though, and for a second too long.

As Jacq Miller's legs finally caved in, Angelina grabbed her under the arms and tried to keep her upright. Unfortunately, Angelina was a slight teenager and Jacq weighed more than a toddler, so both ended up staggering backwards until they hit the desk and fell over.

She felt a flush as the wooden edge jarred into her head. Not only did that *hurt*, Jacq's head wound dripped blood onto her Day Two blouse.

As they slumped together by the desk, there was *another* loud bang from the corner of the room, and Angelina nearly kneed Jacq in the face. It was only Hobson, making an unnecessary amount of noise opening the stairwell door.

"Choi!" He rushed over and levered Jacq up with one arm, propping her against the desk. "You alright?"

"I'm fine, I think." She glanced behind him. "Your boots are covered in blood, what happened?"

"Oh. Fuck. Never mind that, what's *she* doing here?"

"Not sure." Angelina sighed after Jacq stayed silent. "I already called the police though, they'll find out."

"You did *what?*"

"Called the police. Was I not meant to?"

"No! Well, yes, but… just get her to talk, Choi."

"I'm not sure she's up to it, though."

Undeterred, Hobson pointed towards the floor next to Jacq. "Choi. You've been making friends with these people, you're on their wanky wavelength. Get the fuck down there and find out what she knows before Ellie gets here and swoops her away."

"Who's Ellie?"

"Just do it, Choi."

Out of excuses, Angelina sat down next to Jacq and put a sympathetic hand on her arm. The terrified panting rasped to a halt.

"Jacq, hi, you okay?"

"I, um…" At least she didn't faint. "What's going on? What happened?"

"It's Angelina Choi, I'm one of the detectives looking into that murder. What do you, um, remember?"

"I… I…" Jacq felt her own head, a smear of blood came away. "I was turning off the lift just over there, and someone grabbed me from behind and bashed me."

"Bashed you?"

"On the, um, head. I woke up on the second floor, they'd left me there, turned the lift off and stolen my key, then, um, wedged two huge trolleys of rubbish against the entrance. I guess they must've…" Another pause, longer, before her eyes grew to their widest yet. "Oh God, did they rob the place? The owner will be so cross…"

"No, um, nothing taken. I think." She gulped. "So how did you get out?"

"I had a spare lift key in my wallet, I always have a spare, I'm a very careful person. So what did they do? Why did they attack me?"

Another look up, in case Hobson would give some guidance, but he only shrugged. So Angelina spat it out: "They, um, killed Matt, I'm afraid."

Jacq didn't speak another word, just gasped so deep that her belly inflated. Her eyes rolled back into her head and she passed right out, falling onto Angelina's shoulder.

"She's going to blame herself, you know," Angelina murmured as she lowered Jacq to the floor.

"Sure. Fine."

"No need to be so horrible. So what do you think?"

"Not sure. She might've done it, she was here at the time, alibi's bit thin, that gash on her head could be self-inflicted."

"What do you mean she *might've done it*? She totally didn't!"

"Why? Because she's a cuddly lovable flower child who says things like *the owner will be so cross*?"

"Yes! She's not that kind of person!"

"What kind of person? The quiet kind? Matt was quiet, and you spent a day yammering about his secret life as a fucking psycho!"

"That was because…"

The argument was cut short by a burst of sirens from outside. The law, at last. Two police cars, a van full of officers, an ambulance, and more flashing lights behind those.

Hobson took a swift turn to take in the entire room, as if checking what to hide before the teacher comes in. And yet Jacq was the one acting suspicious?

The first police car opened up before it even came to a halt, and a woman in a long coat – much like Hobson's – leapt out and marched straight at the door.

She stopped just inside to look down at the bloody footprints on the floor near the stairwell, and then stared Hobson out for a few seconds. "John. Why have you been stamping through the blood? You didn't think that might contaminate the evidence?"

"It was an emergency."

"I see. So the body's in the stairwell?"

"Yeah."

The policewoman turned away from them both, never even acknowledging Angelina. Seemed rude, considering she'd called 999. After registering the name she'd called Hobson, Angelina looked up at him. "So is this Ellie?"

"Yes, this is Ellie. She's both my ex-wife and a police detective."

"Shit."

EIGHT
LITTLE QUESTIONS

They stood in twitchy silence, watching as the Inspiration Gestation Station filled up with policemen. The cops scraped at the blood on the floor, crowding up the stairwell, bringing in men in white, taping off the lift and door.

Jacq was pulled away by paramedics, but no sign of Matt's remains being moved. Angelina desperately wanted to be gone before the mangled corpse-splat was paraded past her.

Ellie, meanwhile, swooped between gangs of police spitting terse instructions, glancing over at Hobson to ensure he felt out of the loop. The big detective was preoccupied leaning against the desk, looking nonchalant so she knew it wasn't working.

Honestly, it was like Angelina never left her school playground.

At last, Ellie ran out of people to instruct, so came over to them.

"John. Have they searched you and your partner?"

"Yes, Ellie. It was very sexy."

It had not, in fact, been sexy. Angelina was checked over by a woman, but it remained embarrassing. Her most sustained physical contact with anyone besides parents and doctors hadn't lived up to her fantasies.

"Good," Ellie continued, "outside, then. Quickly. And try not to step in any more blood."

They emerged into the small driveway outside the IGS, and Angelina breathed deep. It was a skinny gap between buildings, very quaint and unique in the open air, but in the dark, full of blue lights and with a lake of blood behind her, it felt a lot like an alleyway. A small, dark rut, just about big enough for people to drive round the back to park their cars.

The London air was polluted with exhaust fumes from half a dozen emergency vehicles, but tasted amazing compared to the stale, bloody musk indoors.

Ellie pointed behind a large van. She stood Hobson and Angelina against it and turned to address them like a drill sergeant.

"Okay, you two. I'm told it looks like Matthew Michaelson was killed by a dog again, and although you have many fucking character flaws, John, I can't see any reason or method for you doing this."

"Thanks."

"So, after I've taken statements from you both about what you saw here, you can go. But, and I want to make this as clear as I can: *no more* blundering around crime scenes. To be honest, if you could drop this case entirely, that would be helpful."

"I'll have to consult with my client," Hobson said.

"Fantastic." She gestured to one of her flunkies. "Okay, Sergeant Jensen, take Mister Hobson around the corner while I have a chat to his partner."

Hobson was led off past the front of the van before she could say a word to him. Ellie made eye contact with Angelina for the first time, and she felt cold and small. Her dead-straight hair gave her an air of terrifying severity, along with the big coat and ironed suit. Hobson's black suit seemed increasingly like an affectation, but his ex-wife *owned* it.

"So, Miss Choi, is it?"

"Um, yes."

"Okay, Miss Choi," she said with a surprisingly warm smile, "why don't you tell me what happened here tonight? Don't worry if it makes John Hobson look bad, he does that to himself."

She thought about how best to present the story, but her fear choked all the thoughts at birth. So she opened her mouth and began.

Hobson's wait against the front of the police van, with a large sergeant watching him, was grim. He tried to make small talk about the case, hoping this guy would cough up some forensic results, but no luck. Only a few '*Dunno mate*'s and a lot of stony silence.

So the two of them stood there, picking at their fingernails. Hobson wondered if he could start texting, just as Choi came back around. She looked dazed, but not choked or beaten.

He chanced a few words. "You alright?"

She just nodded.

"Good. Want to head home on your own or wait for me? I'm warning you, pretty sure the papers will be here by now."

Police cars boxed them in, a fair way behind the tape that surrounded the scene. Still, when Hobson and Choi glanced over towards that barrier, the flash and throng of a dozen cameras was visible.

"I'll wait, thanks."

"Fair enough. So, I take it she's ready for me?"

Another small nod.

"Ugh."

"So, you went upstairs, splashed around in the blood a bit, then rushed back down again because you thought your teenage sidekick might be in danger?"

"More or less, Ellie."

"And I suppose the fact you were rushing heroically to save the day means I should let you off for stamping through the evidence?"

"Do what you want."

"John, I'm doing you a favour by not arresting you for tampering with the scene of the crime. The least you could do is not be a prick about it."

"Shit, you're right Ellie. Thanks *ever so* much. Without you, I'm just a stupid arsehole bumbling around playing detective. I don't have a clue what I'm doing and what I need is for a real police dogsbody to show me the light."

"Many a true word spoken in that particular jest, John."

"Such as?"

"Like I'm not sure dragging that kid around with you is helping anyone. She almost cried under interrogation just now. Let her go."

"So you want me to fire Choi and back off the case?"

"Yes. We know what we're doing, we can solve it fine without your *help*."

"I'll think about it."

"I hope so."

"Anything else?"

"Been in any fights lately, John?"

"I'm staying out of trouble."

"Good. Because if people involved in this case start turning up beaten without any claw marks on them, your record means you're our first call."

"I'll be taking my sidekick and leaving, if that's okay Ellie?"

"Of course. Lovely seeing you as ever."

After Angelina stared at the growing paparazzi for a while, the policeman watching her asked if she was okay. She reassured him everything was fine, then tried to look stronger and less troubled.

He didn't look away, this wasn't working. Thankfully, Hobson turned the corner a few minutes later. It felt like his statement was shorter, even though more had happened to him. Maybe he had more experience.

"Choi," he declared as ever, "time to take a walk."

Before sweeping her away, though, he turned to the policeman. "Sergeant, thanks for looking after us. I especially enjoyed the part earlier where you gently touched my inner thigh while searching me."

The tall guy scowled at him and prowled off to rejoin Ellie. Once the police guy's footsteps faded away, the two of them began winding around towards the police line. The media were building up numbers there.

"So, um, Hobson, are we keeping on the case?"

"Damn right. We've got a client, you're in with Social Awesome, we're well on the way."

"But Matt's dead, and the police told us to back off."

"Don't worry, Choi, I didn't pay much attention to her when we were married, I'm sure as fuck not starting now. Not to mention," he said with worrying cheer, "imagine her face when we solve the whole damn thing while she's still pulling dog hairs out of Matt's handstump."

"Okay." Angelina blinked a few times and felt an uncomfortable feeling rising in her stomach. They turned into a bank of flashing cameras and shouting journalists, which only made things worse.

"Choi, say *nothing* to *anyone*. Even *no comment* is too much comment, you get me?"

She nodded, faced front and shoved, because a proper young professional didn't need to be told twice. They waded into the crowd, the road only five or six people away but seeming unreachable, messages smashing into her ears.

"–confirm details of a serial killer–"

"–Twitter detectives at crime scene–"

"–no comment from police at this time–"

"–truth to rumours of wild animal loose in the city–"

"–anything to say to families of victims–"

"–conveniently took this case for free before it escalated–"

"–connections to underground dog fighting–"

"–seedy sex parties gone wrong at Social Awesome–"

"–ex-husband of police detective now walking free from crime scene–"

"–cynical opportunists–"

"–traumatised receptionist was unable to comment–"

"–Edward Lyne and John Hobson, of course, both men with shady pasts–"

"–no interest in justice–"

Dizzy, blinded, Angelina felt a huge hand tug her loose. She still almost staggered over the kerb before Hobson pulled her back from that too.

She turned around to look back at the crowd, unable to process the pushing, shoving mass of hands and noise, long-lens cameras almost jabbing her in the face. In the end, Hobson had to pull her towards the station by the shoulder to get her moving again.

A few opportunistic media types gave chase down the street, but Hobson took a few heavy steps in their direction and they ran away. He didn't even need to clench his fists – skinny journalists trembled at the sight of violence. It made Angelina laugh how utterly terrified some of them were.

Neither Hobson nor Angelina said anything out loud until they reached the train platform and sat down on a bench. Compared to everything else, this seemed like a sanctuary, a precious reserve of boring normality. Drunks meandered along the platform, twitching at passing trains. Sober passers-by, however, were giving them the eyeball. The recognition factor was getting worse.

Nonetheless, Angelina enjoyed being in this completely bland, generic grey station interior. Even the pastel shades of the IGS were too much in her current mood.

Hobson took a long sigh. "Alright, Choi, this is going to be harder than I'd thought, but I reckon we can crack it still."

"You do?"

"Damn straight. We'll be fine. Could you get in early tomorrow? We've got a lot of ground to cover if we're gonna tear this case open."

She just nodded, leaning back against the bench and closing her eyes.

"Good. Oh, and let's try not to finish up the day in this trendy neighbourhood again, eh? It's shit."

Angelina knocked on the door and waited for her mother to unhook the stupid metal bar. Must admit, she'd hoped to get home earlier than this.

As she withdrew from the front door, her mobile began to ring, then immediately stopped. Before she could even check the missed call, the bar clanked off and door flew open, revealing her Mum standing there, hair askew and phone in one hand.

"Angelina," she said with pretend calm, "I've just seen you on the ten o'clock news."

Shit. She forgot her parents sometimes watched TV.

"You told me you were staying out of danger, Angelina. And yet I see you and that massive brute storming out of a building where someone has been *ripped apart* and what on Earth is he thinking?"

"Well, it's not as if I *wanted* to be next to a dead body, I'll try and stay away from that stuff in the future, I promise."

"Not good enough. I'll be calling Mister Hobson *and* your school tomorrow. You can finish your work experience somewhere safer." She snorted to herself. "A prison, perhaps."

"Mum, you can't, it's just getting interesting! You're *ruining* it!"

"Angelina, I don't want to hear another…"

The mobile in her mum's hand started to ring, and she glanced at it mid-reprimand. It tilted enough for Angelina to read *Number Withheld* on the screen.

Giving a clear glare to indicate the shouting would continue after this short break, she took the call. Angelina stomped inside, slamming the door and scowling, while her Mum stuck a finger in one ear to make out the telephone voice. "What was that, sorry?"

Her eyes widened, and she hung up, clamping one hand over the mobile even though it couldn't hear her anymore.

"Angelina," she said, in a flat monotone, "that was a gentleman from the newspapers, asking why I let my teenage daughter hang around bloody murders."

"Oh *fuck*."

"Pardon me, Angelina?"

"Oh... *fiddlesticks*."

Hobson slammed into his office and barged around to his desk, putting his feet up and sighing.

First, he pulled the main office phone cable out. Thank God the press hadn't beaten him back here and set up one of their little refugee camps outside. Next: he tugged his boots off and crashed them together. A fine powder of dried blood drifted into the air, settling in and around the bin. Last of all, he turned on his computer and read online coverage, growing more annoyed with each piece.

This wouldn't do. All the sundry bullshit was getting in the way. He pulled his mobile out – thankfully they didn't yet have this number – and dialled the client.

"Mister Lyne? I hope I'm not disturbing you?"

"I'm fine, Hobson. I assume you're calling about the incident earlier."

"I am. You sad about Matt Michaelson dying?"

"Yes. Finding good programmers is very tedious."

"Interesting answer." He clicked his tongue. "Since your company won't be in the office for a few days, I want you to email the phone numbers and home addresses of all your employees over to me. Include the murdered ones, if you'd be so kind."

"Of course. Anything else?"

"Yeah. I'd like your permission to torture them a little to find out who's doing the killing."

"You think it's someone at Social Awesome?"

"At this point, yeah."

"I suppose so, Mister Hobson. But I've seen some disturbing implications about you on the news, so I have to ask: what kind of *torture* did you have in mind?"

"Strictly hands off, Lyne; no worries. Email the stuff over as soon as you can, ta."

The smiling detective hung up before Lyne could reply. Good to hear the undead-looking batfuck sounding afraid.

NINE
THE PRIVATE LIFE OF VOLES

Been a few years since Hobson last slept in his office – he tried to avoid too many tragic detective clichés.

But after his late night call with Lyne, he'd reclined his chair, leaned back, closed his eyes and let himself slide away. Storming up and down those stairs earlier took more out of him than he'd realised. Soon enough, it was morning, and the sun was tickling his eyelids through the shitty blinds.

His office building might be down to earth and *real* than the twee shared workspace bullshit of the Inspiration Gestation Station, but at least the IGS had window-coverings which might keep out the sun, he thought, prising himself upright in his chair.

The shirt and trousers sweated onto his body in a few awful crevices, legs stiff and the rumbling, chattering sound in his skull felt like the start of a headache. Once he pulled his head from the awful sticky leather, Hobson realised that wasn't the case. It was coming from outside.

Shaking his head, Hobson turned to the computer, still humming away, jerked the mouse to wake the thing up and saw it was already eight.

Despite the creaking pain in his joints, he'd best get to work. Start by dialling the front desk.

"Morning Will. What's that noise? Are the locals demonstrating outside Tesco again?"

"No, Mister Hobson, there's a handful of press waiting at the door. A few of them rang the buzzer and asked to speak to you, but I said you weren't in yet."

"Shit. Could you keep that up please?"

"Of course."

"Thanks Will. You're a good doorman."

He hung up and swore, collapsing his head into his hands.

At seven, Angelina leapt out of bed with her alarm and clicked it off calmly. Her room was tidy, a tasteful shade of lilac with everything filed away into small plastic boxes. Her thoughts were calm. She would not punch her mother.

She lived in a loft conversion at the top of their house – a built-on adjoining palace for the only child. Why take the top floor yourself when you could give it to your teenager? Since she had all this space, best try to keep it tidy. There was an entire bathroom devoted to her – huge amounts of products, all efficiently stored in yet more racks of pastel-coloured boxes.

Calmly, she cleansed herself, rubbing the grease off her face, washing her hair and putting on the bare minimum of make-up. Hobson didn't seem like he had much time for heavy cosmetics. She'd been wearing some eyeshadow on her first day, but even that seemed a lot now she'd met him.

Once ready, she made her way downstairs, swinging around the landing to the bottom floor. Her Mum was already at the dining room table. As Angelina leapt off the final few stairs, thumping into the ground, her Mum marched right out to meet her in the hall. Everything was still, white and cold. The family portrait glared at them.

"Angelina. It's seven thirty, why are you up?"

"Mister Hobson asked me to be in early. Lots to do today," she said, brushing past to get to the cereal.

"You're not going back there, Angelina. Some greasy photographer is hanging around outside. Honestly don't know where these people come from, but you're not going to that office."

"But Mum…"

"Sorry, dear. No."

Angelina clattered her bowl down, trying to stay calm and mannered. "Mum, the police are on the case now, we're just asking some questions, I *promise* it'll be fine, just let me go back to work."

"Angelina, I'm glad you've found something you're passionate about, but there will be other chances."

Staring down her Mum, she could feel the job slipping away. But she had an idea. "Mum. There's a reporter outside, I could go and talk to him."

"Talk to him how?"

"Like about how you and Dad adopted an Asian kid even though you're white so you could… racially abuse me or something."

"You obviously haven't been abused. Don't be silly."

But her eyes widened nonetheless, and Angelina knew she could win. Her Mum liked a quiet life.

"Still, you know what the papers do to suspicious parents in these kind of cases." She stepped away from her breakfast. "You'd be *everywhere.*"

"Angelina, what's gotten into you? Did your detective suggest this?"

"No, he didn't. Let me go back to work with Hobson, please."

"We're your parents, young lady. Don't threaten us."

"You're not my real parents. Can I go back or not?"

Her Mum just glared at her, eyes beginning to redden, before storming from the room without replying. Angelina pulled her coat on, ready to go to work. Only one journalist, according to her mum's report. Stamping straight past him should be easy enough.

"You did *what?"* Hobson sighed. "Choi, I'm not sure whether I'm proud or furious."

There wasn't much he could do about it, though, so he moved the conversation on, flicking through the email Lyne sent him. As promised, full details for every Social Awesome employee. Hobson took a few scrolls up and down before settling on their first stop.

Just as he made the decision, Choi's breathless voice on the phone finally stopped moaning about how difficult this morning had been.

"Okay Choi, that's sad, now, I think I've worked out where we're going. Meet me at Hammersmith station, around 8:45? We're door stepping some suspects."

Once she'd agreed to that, he hung up and started lifting himself out of the damn chair. Time to deal with his own siege situation. Awfully embarrassing if Choi threatened her family to make this meet, but the boss missed it due to a handful of hacks.

Hobson peeked out of the piss-poor blinds to confirm they were still there. He was a detective, not a crime tour guide – might sound like a shit joke, but that was why they were here. Idiot reporters couldn't follow the police around nagging them, but Hobson? Sadly, yes, he was fair game.

Reaching for his coat with one hand, he scrolled down his mobile with the other, until he found the number headed *The Pimp*.

As ever, the call picked up before its first ring even finished.

"Hey hey."

"Yeah, hi. It's John Hobson, I need a favour."

"Man, you finally ready to move on from your ex?"

"Not that kind. Could you have a word with Bible-Amp Benny from outside Peckham Rye and get him over to my building?"

"Benny with the Bible readings and the loudspeaker? Why the fuck? You converting?"

"No, mate. I need him to scare away some idiots from outside."

"No prob, Johnny. And remember, I'm always here if…"

"Thanks. I'm fine."

Hobson hung up, sighed, and locked the office door behind him. Best be ready to make a run for it.

As she emerged from Hammersmith tube, Hobson watched Choi. She peered right back at him, and the pair sized each other up. Neither one cracked and said anything, so he pointed the way and off they went.

After fighting through early ranks of commuters, Hobson reached a peaceful suburb and allowed himself to stroll. No bulking out his shoulders to deflect other pavement users, or kicking the bins.

The next turning led into a square – huge thin townhouses on all sides and garnished with a small park in the middle. Big cars parked around the kerbs, hemmed in to exact spaces, and men in suits marched out towards the main road.

"This, Choi, is rich country." Hobson laughed. "Big houses, posh cars and a park the size of someone's back garden in the middle of your square."

"It's very nice," she mumbled. "So where does Lettie live?"

"With her parents at number twenty, the one with the weird basement entrance and ivy all up the front. You gotta hope they have a dog."

"I thought my parents were doing well with their loft conversion, but this is so… big."

"Doesn't matter after you basically disowned them, does it?"

"I didn't *disown* them, they'll understand."

"You can sleep in my office if you want."

"I'll be fine."

Choi stalked off ahead. She crossed the square, nearly colliding with one blue-suited passer-by, before slowing again at the bottom of the stone steps to the destination. They were big, wide and substantial, like the Voles wanted their home to be some mighty Aztec temple. The multiple stories of redbrick house shot up, like some aspiring skyscraper. Hobson arrived and put his foot right onto the bottom step.

"So what do we *say* to them?" Choi asked.

"Follow my lead, Choi. It'll be easy."

Hobson crashed past her, up the steps, lifted his hand and rapped on the door. Curtains twitched all around the square, loud thumps floating from corner to corner, but at least there were no bloody tabloid reporters.

A moment later, the door opened and Mrs Vole appeared in the doorway, as if she'd been standing there all along. The mother of the Vole household was as tall and ginger as both her children, but wider and, unbelievably, even angrier.

The shout of *"What do you two want?"* made an even bigger commotion than Hobson knocking. Her roar rolled through the park, causing some of the curtain-twitchers to stop hiding and lean out of their windows.

Hobson was determined not to seem impressed.

"Mrs Vole? I'm John Hobson, investigating the murders at your daughter's job. We're here to talk to Violet?"

"I know who you are, Mister Hobson," she said, sniffing. "You're the one on the news."

"I am that."

"The policewoman on TV said you'd be dropping the case soon for the good of the families."

"I'm sure she did," Hobson said. "If we could just speak to your daughter?"

Mrs Vole scowled. "No. Please leave."

The door whipped shut, nearly smacking him in the face. That sound was echoed by a string of windows crashing closed as Hobson turned around, like slow machine gun fire.

"And this, Choi, is why modern media is bullshit. I am never taking another case like this again."

"I know, it's my fault, I'm sorry, but we're so close, aren't we? We can't stop now, I can feel it…"

"Wait." Hobson held up a hand to her, a flat **STOP** signal, and zeroed in on a high-pitched rustle. "That sobbing noise. It's not you secretly crying, is it?"

"No…"

When she stopped talking, Angelina could hear it too – a heaving, weeping sob, coming from below the stone ascent to the doorway. Underneath was a dip of concrete with steps cut in, descending to a small messy garden. It was like a vine-filled prison cell, a wooden door into some mysterious lower room buried at the back.

Hanging out of there, listening to every word they were saying, was Lettie Vole. "Angie?"

"Lettie?" Angelina jumped back to the street, scuttled down the concrete stairs through a hanging cloud of plants, crunched through mud and leaves. Brushing them away with one hand, she reached out to grab Lettie's shoulder.

"Are you okay, Lettie? You heard about Matt?"

Her face was bright, she shook a little. Hobson had enough sense to keep back.

"Yeah, um, yeah. Angie, what happened? They said you were there?"

"Well, I was hiding under a desk, to be honest. Hobson, he was, um, more there than me."

"He said he was just going to meet you then he'd see me later. He wouldn't tell me why." Lettie's teeth gritted and she assumed her more familiar expression of flat rage. "How the *fuck* did he end up dead with you two right there?"

"I'm sorry Lettie," she said. "I wish we could've done… something. I think it must've happened before we even arrived, isn't that right Hobson?"

Angelina looked back up towards the street, and there was the response: "Yeah, I reckon so. The dog was on him a while before we arrived. The twat had legged it."

Lettie coughed, then retreated back into her house. Angelina looked back to Hobson, who only narrowed his eyes and jabbed towards the open door.

Lacking a better idea, she followed Lettie inside. This bottom room in the house was furnished with battered sofas, messy piles of boxes covered in dust and a small TV in the corner – this clearly wasn't the main entertaining area. The boxes were full of old books and board games, tidy but not neat.

Lettie herself sprawled along one of the sofas, arms behind her head. Angelina went over to her, as Hobson entered the tiny dip with a flurry of snapping twigs and ducked to get under the doorway. He knocked his head anyway and cursed.

"So, um, are you okay?" Angelina tried. "You seem to be taking this hard."

"Yeah, you just don't expect this sort of fucking thing in your own office, do you?" Lettie growled.

Hobson passed through the room to poke around in the adjacent kitchen, pulling his phone from his pocket as he went. Angelina ignored him and tried to keep Lettie talking.

"No, I suppose you don't," she said.

"I mean, why bother doing all this?" said Lettie. "Taking a dog up and down a building, killing programmers who never hurt anyone just because, what, bored? Pissed off with their boss?"

"You think it's someone trying to hurt Lyne?"

"Look, either it's someone trying to get him, or it *is* him. His fucking fault, one way or the other. Fucker."

"Maybe, maybe."

Angelina's phone beeped and she checked it on reflex. It was a text from Hobson in the next room: *Ask her why she said she'd see Matt later that night.*

"Um, why did you say you'd see Matt later last night, anyway?"

"What?"

"Outside just now, you said you were meeting him after he'd seen us."

Angelina sensed Hobson looming in the kitchen doorway behind her.

"Oh, um, we were just going for a drink. Or a movie, you know, he was a nerd, he liked movies, in fact he…"

A quiet exhale of annoyance escaped Hobson's lips. "Okay, were you two fucking?"

Eyes wide with fury, Lettie leapt up from her sofa. Angelina turned on him as well, her own face going the same way.

"He's dead, how fucking *dare* you." Lettie marched round the room. "He's dead because you couldn't solve the crime, or you're working for Lyne, maybe you're helping him avoid getting caught, and you come round here…."

"But you were," Hobson made a visible effort to moderate his language. "Seeing each other? Something like that?"

Her shoulders slumped and another brief sob escaped her. Angelina inched closer, unsure whether she would get punched.

"Yes. Something like that. Not for long, though."

"Okay. Thank you. Can I just ask a few questions about…?"

A heavy stamp crashlanded in the kitchen, as Mrs Vole made her way down from the upper floors. "Are you two down there? I thought I told you to get lost!"

At the same time, Hobson's phone rang. He checked the screen, swore, then picked up the call anyway. "Ellie? What is it?"

He stepped away towards the back door, leaving Angelina to deal with yet another angry mother.

"Hi, sorry, Lettie, um, Violet let us in down here, I think she just wanted to talk about…"

"If she needs to talk, she can talk to me. Or the police *or* a psychologist, just not you people. Now *get out* before I have you arrested."

Just as the police were mentioned, Hobson yelled into his phone: "You've *arrested* Edward Lyne? What the fuck? He was my client."

"Were you not listening? *Leave!*" screamed Mrs Vole.

For a few moments, as Mrs Vole shoved herself into Hobson's face while his ex-wife hung up on him, he lost touch with the outside world. His ears felt walled off, a solid burst of white sound tunnelled in, and all he could hear, all he could feel, was a silent screaming. Trapped in this dusty, unused cave below a house, he felt it squeezing him.

His fingers twitched, and he wondered if clamping his hand over the yelling woman's mouth was an option. She'd pushed his tiny assistant out of the way, the daughter was standing to one side wailing, nothing remained between them.

Just as his forearm was tightening to lift, Lettie yelled out: "HEY!"

Hobson turned to her. "Yeah?"

"Did you say they'd arrested Mister Lyne?"

"That's the news."

A grim smile spread across her face, accentuated by the perpetual scowl. "Good. He deserved it."

"He *was* a bit of a twat, but ain't sure he deserved this specific thing."

"Wait," Mrs Vole turned down the volume to face her daughter, "your boss killed those kids?"

"Yes," said Lettie.

"No," said Hobson

"Maybe," she conceded.

His patience exhausted, Hobson caught Choi's eye and gestured towards the door. She went for it in silence; the noise seemed to have scared her mute.

He turned back. "Lettie, did your boss know about your sexual relationship with the deceased? It's relevant, I promise."

"Um, no. Not that I'm aware."

"Cheers, Violet. We'll leave you in peace now, ladies, thanks for your time."

Mrs Vole's glare turned on her daughter as Hobson swept away to duck out of that basement. The yelling started before they'd finished climbing the stairs to the street.

Choi scurried along behind, brushing specks of leaf and dust off her coat. She looked up at him once finished. "You know her Mum's going to give her hell about that."

"Oh, is she? Whoops."

"Did you really need to say *sexual*?"

"Maybe I didn't *need to*, Choi, but I do enjoy it, y'know?"

"Ugh."

"You're just jealous because she still has a Mum to yell at her."

Choi stormed off, making it a fair way back towards the station before turning back to ask Hobson where they were going.

TEN
THE QUIET ONES

Despite Angelina complaining it was distasteful, Hobson called the hospital pretending to be Jacq's father to ask if she'd been discharged yet. Thanks to the high profile nature of the case, several journalists already tried that one. The nurse hung up.

Not easily discouraged, Hobson instead phoned a couple of reporters, pretending to be one of their colleagues. They coughed up the information soon enough: Jacqueline Miller sent home mid-morning, a few stitches but nothing more serious, no brain damage, quite upset.

Hobson grinned at Angelina over his mobile. "And released into the care of one Emily Allen. I'm guessing they went to Emily's place, she'd definitely fake being too hopeless to look after herself. Slots right into her pissweak persona."

"You still think she's hiding something?"

"You bet."

"Surely she couldn't hurt anyone, though? I mean, she's just too nice?"

"Have to wait and see, won't we?"

"So we're going over there?"

"Obviously."

Before she could argue any more, a skinny man in a baggy shirt and small glasses came over to their table. He'd been sitting nearby, and Angelina thought she'd spotted a couple of looks over. She'd liked how self-assured and cool he seemed, even if about ten years older than her. Disappointing to discover he'd only been after one thing: "Mister Hobson? Ross Watts, Evening Star. Any comment on the arrest of your employer?"

"None."

"Any comment on the rumour that the real reason you've been hired is to clean up after Edward Lyne's crimes?"

"No."

"Any comment on what's with the tiny Asian girl?"

Both Hobson and Watts looked at Angelina for a moment, and she did her best to glower with authority. Hobson turned back to the journalist, not smiling at all.

"No comment at all, you four-eyed beanpole fuckwit. Choi," he pointed to the exit, "let's go see these girls."

They snuck into Emily's building when someone else left the door swinging a little too long. Angelina wanted to ring the doorbell like a normal person, but Hobson wasn't doing that. "If we only went where we were wanted, Choi," he said, smug as ever, "we'd be sitting in my office doing the fuckin' crossword."

They swept into the foyer, past the notice board and up the stairs for the flat number Lyne had given them: number twenty-two. As they marched up the grey, stained stairwell, Angelina shivered at the thought of poor Matt, dying alone in a similar boring column. Ridiculous, of course, she'd barely seen it happen.

Whereas Hobson splashed through Matt's blood with his own two boots, yet bounced up these stairs without a care in the world.

They reached the second floor and there were two flats: twenty-one and twenty-two. Not missing a step, nor consulting with his assistant about how to approach this sensitive conversation, Hobson pounded on the door.

After no-one responded, Angelina piped up. "Hobson, maybe we should leave them be. They might be at Jacq's place."

"Nah. Wouldn't fit the cover story." He hammered the door some more, adding a yell. "Emily, it's John Hobson! Open up!"

The lock crunched, door shot a few degrees open, revealing an angry Emily standing in the gap. "What do you two want?"

"Hi, Emily." Angelina waved, remembering she was the one with connections.

"Yeah, hi. What do you two want?"

"Is Jacq here?" Hobson said, straight to business.

"Maybe."

"We were wondering if we could ask her a few questions about what happened back at the office."

"Weren't you both right there?" Emily said.

"She was there earlier, though."

"I don't think she's up to it."

"Come on, look, Mister Lyne wants us to sort all this out. Give us a few minutes and we'll be out of your hair. Don't you *want* to catch whoever killed Matt?"

Emily's hand twitched on the edge of her door, as if weighing up smashing it into his face, but she nodded in the end. "Okay. Fine."

Angelina wondered if she knew Edward Lyne had been arrested. Possibly not, as the door flew open without a word about it, allowing them to step into her spotless blue-painted corridor.

"So, um, bad news about Matt, isn't it?" Angelina had another go at connecting with Emily as they pulled their coats off.

"He was a harmless enough guy, I suppose."

"Did you know he was dating Lettie?"

"Really? Wow. I suppose it had been a while since he asked me out. At least he wasn't *too* weird about it."

"He seemed a *bit* weird."

"Well, at least he didn't stare at my tits as blatantly as Pete."

"Yeah, I know, I hate it when people stare at my, um, yeah."

Angelina trailed off her attempt to sound grown-up, feeling a blush spread upwards. She couldn't help but notice Hobson and Emily exchanging smiles.

They faced the door on the left. Emily put a hand on the doorknob and paused, all trace of amusement dropping away. "Could you please try and be nice? Jacq hasn't been great since it happened, okay?"

"We'll be charming," said Hobson, "now let's get to it."

Not looking reassured, Emily leaned into the door. It swung open to reveal a decent-sized front room, with two sofas, a huge window, more of that blue colour and a medium TV. There were a few bland paintings up, a toy teddy bear on the mantelpiece. Finishing off the decor, sprawled across one sofa, was Jacqueline Miller.

Her pyjamas were sweated through and baggy – probably borrowed from the bigger Emily – curly hair clinging together, moaning in fitful sleep.

Angelina drew away. "Hobson, maybe we *should* come back later."

She never got to hear a reply, as Jacq lurched up from the sofa like a zombie. She turned to see the two of them, then started panting, breathing heavily and yelling, eyes fluttering, legs finally moving to the edge of the sofa and wrecking her balance. As she tumbled backwards onto the floor, Emily rushed around to check she was okay.

"Fuck me," Hobson muttered, "my contact said there wasn't any brain damage. And why do people keep bloody wailing at us today?"

"What's wrong with her?" Angelina muttered.

"Looks like trauma." He scratched his head. "She's either a *really* sensitive soul, or she's over-acting the shit out of it."

"And which one do you think it is?"

"What do you fuckin' think?"

Watching Emily coax Jacq back onto the sofa was boring Hobson rigid. And not in the good way.

First, they talked on the floor for a while, then Emily helped Jacq stand up, and *then* she needed hours of assistance to lie down again. How could the basic act of falling over take so long? Didn't these women know he had better things to do?

Hobson realised Choi was glaring at him.

"Yes? What's wrong?

"You're tapping your foot and muttering, could you try not to? Must be very pressuring for poor Jacq."

"*Poor Jacq* my arse."

"Charming."

After a few minutes of work, Emily had Jacq comfortable again. She looked disappointed to see Hobson and Choi were still there.

"Okay," Emily said, "I suppose you can talk to her now. If you must."

"About time."

She stepped back to let them file around Jacq's sofa. Hobson loomed overhead, while Choi sat down near her legs. Jacq was staring straight ahead, pale as anything, eyes wide, off-white dressing on her head where they'd sewn it shut. Curly hair splayed all around her, limp and washed out.

Looking down at Jacq, as she gazed back like a poor, helpless injured bird, Hobson scowled, trying to get *some* reaction. Any rumble of vicious anger which might hint that her helplessness was all faked. Taking his silence as a cue to move in, Choi leaned closer and started the interview herself.

"So, um, Jacq, I'm Angelina, do you remember me? And this is Hobson?"

She nodded, Hobson grunted.

"Do you remember we were investigating the murders?"

Another faint nod.

"Look, we don't want to upset you, but can we ask you some questions about Matt dying?"

"Yes. Of course, I want to help."

"Okay. Do you have any idea who ambushed you in the lift that night?"

"Um, I don't know. Big hands, I think, breathing sounded like a man, but he might've had the dog with him, I couldn't remember."

"That's good, thanks." Angelina grabbed her hand. "Do you have any idea who might want to hurt Matt *and* William Lane?"

"Matt was awkward, William never really fitted in, maybe… I don't know, Matt was so harmless, he kinda reminded me of me. Do you think they blame me?"

"Who?"

"Matt's family. I was on reception, I should've been guarding the building against stuff."

"I don't think anyone was expecting you to fight off serial killers with attack dogs, Jacq." Angelina squeezed her fingers. "You did fine."

"I told them I could handle it. I said I was stronger than I looked, it would all be fine, but first difficult situation and it all just went…"

"That's enough." The tears were starting again. Emily moved around behind Angelina, stooping into her eye line and pointing towards the front door. "I hope that helped, but you're upsetting her. Time to go."

"Okay." Angelina looked up at Hobson. "Anything else?"

He just shook his head, letting Emily usher them out of her flat. Their host didn't say anything else, just held her front door open for as little time as possible, then shut it behind them. Once they were back in the stairwell, Angelina turned to Hobson.

"What happened to you in there?"

"I don't know what to tell you, Choi. I didn't realise she was this badly fucked. Didn't realise people actually were this twee and sensitive, to tell you the truth."

"So you thought she was faking everything about herself?"

"That's more or less the size of it. God, wouldn't life be easier if we just killed all the hipsters?"

"She's not a hipster, she's just quiet."

"Whatever the fuck she is, Choi. Whatever the fuck."

It was a shade after lunchtime when they stopped in yet another local sandwich shop. Hobson was willing to settle for non-branded vendors if he couldn't find a Subway. They sat at the back, on the other side of the counter and its ice cream boxes full of fillings, shielding themselves from the vultures.

"So, ready to give up on *it's always the quiet ones* yet?" Choi said.

"Because it wasn't Matt and probably isn't Jacq?"

"Yeah."

"Maybe." He sighed. "Still think it's one of them from that company, though."

"Or we're coming at it all wrong and it's a business associate of that dog-fighting guy getting revenge for his death."

"Maybe if the second victim had been Pete or Ric, no reason to come after the colleagues though. I still think it's got to be Social Awesome. Instincts bitchslapping me."

"So if it's not the quiet ones, maybe it's the obviously evil boss?"

"Yeah." Hobson took another bite of his sandwich. "Maybe all you people are right and it *is* him."

Choi was in the middle of a smug moment when she caught sight of the TV, flickering away in the corner of the sandwich bar. "Hey, speaking of the literal devil."

Hobson had to bend his neck all the way around to see it, but there was the news. The two sandwich preparation artists gazed at it, not even trying to disguise their boredom.

"…Edward Lyne released from police custody, charges dropped for now…"

On that, Hobson couldn't stop himself bursting out laughing. "Fuck a duck, is Ellie enforcing the law by flipping a coin now? That's gotta hurt. Poor bitch."

"That's not very nice."

"If she's going to arrest people on sketchy evidence because they look dodgy, she deserves everything she gets. I think I'm gonna go see him."

"Aren't we doing a Social Awesome tour? Next stop Pete and Ric, surely?"

"Those two arseholes? We can do them tomorrow."

"Or I can do them now."

"Nah, go home, Choi. You should get back at a reasonable time and without anyone dying. Don't want your parents to properly disown you."

"You don't need to worry, I can take care of myself."

"By going round to hang out with the boys?" He caught her eye, making sure to smile as she looked away. "*Home*, Choi. We'll do them tomorrow, if I can't get Lyne to confess now."

"So now your ex-wife's let him go, you've decided you want to prove he did it after all?"

"Shut up. *Home.*"

ELEVEN
HEAD TO HEAD

"What's the matter, Mister Hobson? Surprised I don't sleep in a coffin?"

"Heh." Hobson looked around Lyne's tiny hallway, struggling to fit. "A little."

Coming to meet the well-tailored Social Awesome owner, Hobson expected his second towering townhouse of the day, a skinny four-floored monster like the Vole property. Instead, he was whisked up in a lift so clean he daren't touch the sides, rising to a flat with nothing but shiny surfaces. Not even a rug as a comfortable pause. Well, at least he could be certain Lyne had a reflection.

The reception area behind the door was small, but soon morphed into a huge room. It was bigger than the Social Awesome office or Hobson's entire home, one wall occupied only by a gigantic window. Before entering this cushy building, Hobson resolved to be unimpressed, but this was luxury he'd only ever seen in films.

The evening was settling in by now, it was cold outside – not in here, obviously – and they were in the outskirts of Canary Wharf. The part of East London where the wealthy held off the young and trendy by pricing them out of the market. The view was amazing, as long as you liked modern architecture. Skinny towers, fat blocks, glass and brick, standing firm against the fingers of sunset. A thousand panes of glass, a few people working hard in suits behind them, a million lives. If Hobson lived here, he could work from a sofa facing the window with a pair of binoculars, sending Choi out for occasional sandwiches.

Anyway, Lyne was talking to him. "Drink, Mister Hobson?"

"Got a beer?"

"Of course."

"Go on then."

Lyne reached into his fridge and pulled out two cold bottles – it occurred to Hobson this host would always take the same as his guest, no matter what the depraved drink order. They moved over towards two leather chairs pointed at the middle-sized TV. These were the closest to softness in the room, but still glistened. Hobson sat down and almost sighed out loud from the comfort. Lyne settled into the chair across from him, curled his thin legs up and stared at Hobson from small, black eyes.

Hobson cracked his beer open, and gave a friendly nod in lieu of a toast. Decent brand of drink; not too common or too trendy. This guy knew what he was doing.

"So, Mister Lyne…"

"I think we can finally get down to first names, can't we?"

"Okay then, *Edward*." He forced *Edward* out, even though it didn't sound right. "What the hell happened? Why did the police grab you?"

"The same reason you treat me like a Bond villain, I suppose. Everyone hates someone who ignores the niceties of how things *should* be and just tries to make a living."

"So not because you've been knocking off your employees with a giant dog?"

"John, why would I bother? I can fire them, I've set up their contracts to make that easy. Having them killed draws attention."

When Lyne said *John*, Hobson noted, it sounded natural. "So you didn't have any business secrets you wanted hushed up? Nothing like that at all?"

Lyne's creepy smiling calm cracked and he looked away for a moment, gazing out over the sky. "So you heard we're not all we seem?"

"I gathered your company is some kind of halfarsed con-job and William Lane was considering outing you, if that's what you're fucking referring to."

"Yes."

"As if I didn't know it was all bullshit as soon as I heard the name *Social Awesome*. Was that why you were arrested? Someone pass that on to the cops, did they?"

"Indeed. Obviously, it was Violet Vole." His expression didn't flicker as he said that. "Considering I employed her as a favour to her brother, she's rather rude and ungrateful."

"That is a bit of an arse-ache, Edward. Maybe you should have your dog rip her into pieces, or some such similar shit."

"John, please. It wasn't me."

"Urgh. This case is such a clusterwank. Maybe it was all Violet Vole and she's trying to cover her tracks."

"I think she's just stroppy, John."

"You're probably right. Doubt she'd have killed Matt if she was doing him."

"Violet Vole was sleeping with Matt Michaelson?" Lyne sat up, spine straight for the first time in minutes. "I thought she was seeing Pete's surviving housemate."

"Ric? That guy with the hair? He's a prick."

"As is Violet Vole."

"Fair point."

But even as he bantered, Hobson's internal computer clicked, hummed and spun. He flickered through his thoughts drawing conclusions, and glancing at the other guy, could see Lyne doing the same.

"So," he muttered to break the silence, "we're both on the same lines, yeah?"

"That considering they both lived uncomfortably with the first victim and had reasons to resent the second, Pete Vole and Ric McCabe are now our most likely suspects?"

"Christ, Edward, I don't have a sister, but would you kill someone because he was sleeping with her? That's fucked up."

"I do have a sister, and I must admit, if I disapproved of the suitor enough, I might consider it."

"Fuck me. It's always this way, isn't it?"

"How do you mean, John?"

"I mean, with the big murder cases, the messy ones in real life or on TV or *whatever*. It's never just about corporate intrigue or some shit, is it? It always ends up being about Violet Vole's vagina."

"I'm not sure it's always that *specific* vagina."

"You're probably right. Ah well. Maybe we can wrap this shit up at last."

"That would be delightful, John. I'm looking forward to getting my business back underway. Shall we call the police and tell them our suspicions?"

"No." Hobson's voice came out as such a bark, Lyne laughed. "Let's sort it out before calling the filth. I want to turn up at their damn donut station with the right guy, a file of cast-iron evidence and the dog trotting in front of me on a lead."

"Any particular reason?"

"I'm a right conscientious detective."

"Fair enough."

He stood up from the chair, even though it was amazing, and wondered if he could break in later and steal it. Best focus on the murders for now.

"Edward, I'd best be on my way, you've given me a lot to think about." Hobson handed him back the beer bottle, with another nod and the thinnest of smiles. "I can let myself out. I'll let you know what happens."

"I'd appreciate it, John."

Hobson strode out of the flat, squeezing himself through the corridor. As he stepped back into the lift, pausing for another glance through the window, he pulled out his mobile. Choi answered quickly, sounding nervous.

"Hey, kid. Got news straight from the evil horse's nosebag."

The lift doors hummed shut.

"You can't talk because you're *where?* Fucking where? What did I tell you about going there? Jesus Christ."

It swept towards the ground, nowhere near quick enough for Hobson's liking.

"Okay, look, don't reckon I should tell you anything now, *get out* and text me a place to meet you, okay?"

"Good. Good. Fuck."

With that, he hung up, and wondered if a huge chap jumping up and down might make this lift accelerate. It was risky, so he put it aside for the moment. Maybe he should call the police, though?

Angelina sat, phone still clasped to her ear, a good ten seconds after Hobson finished swearing and hung up. She was silent for so long, Ric looked perturbed.

"Hey, you alright there, Angelina? What's wrong?"

She tried to shake herself out of it. "Um, yeah, Mister Hobson sent me to talk to you about the, um, murders."

"I guessed. Was that him? Did he grunt something and then swear at you for asking about it?"

"Um, he didn't say much. Did you say Pete was home too?"

"Oh yeah," Ric pointed towards his living room ceiling, "he's up there, don't worry. Probably crying about Emily or something. Soon he'll be down and then we can get this sorted."

"Actually, well, it's late, my parents have worried about me since, um, that thing with Matt, y'know, maybe I should just get going instead."

"You've only just arrived, come on, stay for a while. We never get any visitors since William got himself eaten."

Ric had dyed his hair a deep black since Angelina had last seen him. She couldn't decide if this was cool or unsettling. He wasn't helping matters by smiling like a hungry wolf.

"Ellie, you there?"

"John?"

"Yeah, can you get some uniform gimps over to Pete and Ric's house?"

"Please don't refer to the dedicated men and women of the Met as 'uniform gimps'."

"Fucking hell, okay, the house where you found William Lane, can you get some *people* over there? I think Choi might be in danger."

"Your intern?"

"Yes. I think one or more of them two pricks might be the killer. I'd appreciate someone getting there before she discovers the dark side of dogging."

"That's horrible."

"Just do it, for Christ's sake."

"Got any evidence for this claim?"

"Probably more than you did when you arrested Lyne."

"For fuck's sake, John."

"*For fuck's sake, Ellie*, you're meant to be the law. Get over there before she gets eaten."

"Okay, enough. I'll sort it out."

"Thank you. I'm getting on the tube now. See you there."

"Goodbye John."

Pete entered, and Angelina gulped. He looked dishevelled, sweaty, rubbing his arms inside a thick sweater as if he couldn't stop feeling cold. His angular face pointed down at her like an arrow. She preferred it when he tried too hard to flirt with her, honestly. Even Ric's bright sarcasm and goth-haired grin diminished as the sulking presence drifted into their living room.

"Evening, Pete. What's up?" he said, on the off chance his housemate felt like chatting.

But Pete just indicated Angelina with a thumb. "Why's she here? I thought we'd agreed not to talk to anyone."

"Oh, I know we're not talking to the papers, but we know her, don't we? She's partners with the big grumpy one."

"Hobson, yeah. The man who protected us so well, Matt died while he was downstairs."

"Hey, Matt was dead when we got there, it's not our fault."

Pete made a great show of sitting down on the side of her dusty armchair. "What was that? You think I should let you off for being fucking useless?"

"No, I just don't think… I mean, we weren't there to *protect* you really…"

"My housemate is dead, my sister's boyfriend as well…"

"So you knew Lettie and Matt were seeing each other, then?"

The two men exchanged glances, before Pete carried on talking. "Well, yeah. Lettie isn't as good a spy as she thinks, and Matt can't keep a secret at all."

"And what do you guys think about the two of them?"

"Well, y'know, I thought Matt was a bit creepy and awkward to tell you the truth, but whatever makes her happy. Well, *made* her happy. At least Matt moved on from gazing at Emily."

"And how about you, Ric?"

"Um," Ric seemed lost for words, "I suppose I'm a little jealous. I mean, Lettie's a decent catch, not sure how she ended up with a guy who got whiplash whenever he looked up from the floor."

"I see." Angelina nodded. She also spotted Pete darting his eyes towards Ric when he referred to Lettie as *a decent catch.*

The small, brown living room seemed more and more cramped. It was getting hard to ignore the fact there were two of them, both bigger than her, and Pete was right up close, scowling and fidgeting. Angelina preferred it when he'd been uncomfortably familiar – at least she hadn't feared for her safety.

"So go on then?" He jeered at her. "Whodunnit? Found anything useful?"

"I…"

"I'm sure she just needs more time." Ric cut in. "Not to mention: at this rate, there'll only be one Social Awesome employee left by next week. That one will definitely be the killer."

"Thanks." She nodded to him, chancing a smile.

"No worries."

He smiled right back and Pete, seeing this exchange, rolled his eyes, levering himself off the chair with a heavy sigh. Angelina flinched away despite herself.

"I'll leave you two to it then. Glad everyone's deaths could bring you together. And glad you're not lingering too much over my sister Ric, not when there's some fucking slant-eyed jailbait handy."

And before anyone could comment, he'd stormed back the way he came, ascending the stairs with maximum noise, leaving both Angelina and Ric gaping after him. Moments later, his bedroom door slammed.

"So, um, was that…." She trailed off.

"Yeah," Ric picked it back up, "that was uncomfortably racist. Not sure what's happened to Pete lately, sorry."

"Lately… Has he been weird and moody since people started dying, then?"

"Well, kinda quiet, angry, comes and goes, leaves his dirty plates in my sink, refuses to wash them. Sometimes I wonder if…"

"Yes?"

Angelina was on the edge of her seat, when there was a string of crashing noises at the front door, seeming to shake the house.

"You two arseholes! Get out here and check yourself before you shit yourselves!"

The spell broken, Ric stared in the direction of the sound, looking like he feared for his life. "Is that…?"

"Yeah, that's my boss. But don't worry, he's not really going to…"

"Hand over my intern before I show that guy's hair a new shade of red!"

"Okay, we should open the door before he hurts himself."

Ric showed no sign of moving. Angelina sighed, leapt over the arm of her chair and threw herself into the corridor. Before she went for the front door, she glanced up the stairs to check for movement from Pete. Nothing – the whole upper floor was in darkness.

She went to let Hobson in, just as his latest round of punching noises started up. He was so surprised by the door swinging open, a fist fired past the gap and over his intern's shoulder, brushing through her hair. Angelina stood firm and stared him down as he retracted the arm.

"Do you mind?"

His whole body relaxed, fists dropping to his side. "Choi. Everything okay?"

"Under control. Are *you* okay?"

"Not sure. Might've over-reacted a tad."

Angelina sidestepped to look around his huge shoulder. Five uniformed police fanned out behind him, along with Ellie. She wore her own sweeping coat and looked unimpressed.

"You brought the police?"

"I'm *sure* one of these guys is this dog-killer."

"Oh."

Ric crept out from behind Angelina. "Is everything okay? Have they got the wrong house in a drug bust?"

"Not sure yet."

"You there, smug little prick." Hobson spat that out on sight.

"Hobson, try to be nice."

"Choi, I'll be nice when I'm dead. Now, Ric McCabe: you didn't like your housemate and resented Matt for sniffing around Lettie Vole. Did you kill them?"

"No, sorry. I've never been good with animals, they give me the sneezies."

Angelina's shoulders slumped.

Hobson turned around to his ex-wife. "Detective Ellie! Arrest McCabe *and* Vole until we work out which one it is."

"No, John. Sorry."

"Can't you at least nab that one for obstructing justice by making shit jokes?"

"Tempting, but probably not."

"Also," Angelina piped up, "if it's either of them, it's Pete. He was being horrible earlier, and Ric said he's been like that since this started."

All eyes turned to Ric. "Um, I don't wanna get him in trouble. He was just weirded out."

"Oh my God, you're useless!" Angelina turned around and screamed at him, as most of the watching policemen burst out laughing. A few neighbours chuckled on their doorsteps.

Just like that, it was over. Ellie turned to her men. "Okay guys, we haven't got enough on either of them yet. Since Miss Choi is unharmed, we're out for now."

They went back for their vehicles, Hobson and Angelina staring wide-eyed at the idiocy, as Ric slammed the door to his house. For a moment, it looked like Ellie was going to come over and say something to Hobson, but even that didn't happen. Total anti-climax. She merely shot him a look before leaving with the other policemen, their space on the pavement quickly filled in by the ever-present lingering infection of the press.

Hobson's efforts to avoid sleeping in his office were not going well. This was the second night in a row, but at least he curled up on the floor rather than passing out in a chair.

But the feeling of progress was a hollow one, especially after his mobile phone woke him at eight in the morning. Not the alarm either, but a proper phone call from Ellie. Would she finally order him point-blank to get off the case?

Eyes still closed, he took the call.

"Ellie, hi."

"John, we've got another body in the dog case."

Now he was awake. "Fuck me. Who?"

"Edward Lyne."

"Ripped to giblets again?"

"In his flat, yes. You can come have a look if you think you've got anything to add, please don't bring the kid."

"I thought you wanted me to fuck off to save the families?"

"You seem to be more in with these people than us. I need something to show the boss after that Edward Lyne fuck-up."

"No worries. Although I will say, *the kid* is more in with Social Awesome than I am."

"Don't push it, Hobson."

"Sorry. Any chance we can pin it on Pete or Ric?"

"That's the thing, John," she sounded disappointed, "after you were so emphatic about your suspicions, I put men on their house and we're pretty sure they didn't leave all night."

"So it wasn't…"

"Looks that way."

"Oh *fuck*."

TWELVE
CRUSTY SEMEN INSPECTORS

Ten in the morning, Angelina in yet another cafe. She'd guessed becoming a detective's assistant would involve hanging around, but honestly, she might buy a Kindle. At least she could catch up on her reading.

Not to mention, another gadget would help her fit in against this particular eatery. It was a chain she'd never heard of near Canary Wharf, among a cluster of shining buildings resembling mirrors. All the sandwiches were paninis, the coffees had Italian names, punters looked like cartoons of bankers. She'd dressed up, worn a suit jacket and her most expensive black skirt, but still felt like a pleb.

She ignored them, stared at her coffee, updated Twitter and fiddled with the black radio box in her hand. It connected to her ears and the microphone clipped to her shirt.

"Hobson? Testing, testing, testing? You in there yet?"

Her boss' voice was a low bass rumble making her skull shake. "Calm it down, Choi. This lift wants to take its own sweet fuckin' time while I check out the shiny walls."

"Okay okay, sure."

She glanced across the tables to see how many people were staring at her: only three so far. Good start. Even though it wouldn't stop them looking, she started talking again to take her mind off it.

"Why are we using this microphone thing, anyway? You can get apps for this on smartphones if you'd just buy one. Seriously, like an old-fashioned walkie-talkie app, where you hold down a button and speak, that sort of thing. It's awesome, kinda retro-cool, y'know?"

"Choi, please stop trying to sell me mobile phones, it's just embarrassing."

"Fine."

"Good. Now, get ready to have useful feedback. We're here."

And through her earpiece, Angelina heard the lift doors sweep open.

There wasn't much blood in the lift, Hobson noted. It looked like the serial killer and their dog managed to keep things clean, rather than leave a spattering of gore for him wallow in.

As he stepped back out into the bright, tasteful hall, the door to Lyne's flat already open, he readied himself for crimson spill. To his surprise, not a drop here either. Nothing in the doorway, or anywhere else, not even any spilt at the lift exit while trying to escape. The lock was unbroken, no cops examining it.

"Not much blood in the hallway, Choi," he said into the mike, "looks like they've finally taught the pooch some manners."

"You think they're getting careful?" she murmured back.

"Either that or they left Lyne's flat by abseiling out the fuckin' window, or parachuting, or they're still hiding in the…"

A sharp cough stopped Hobson mid-hypothesis. It was Ellie, leaning out from the flat doorway and already looking weary. "John, I thought I said leave the kid at home."

She glanced around the hallway. Hobson smiled and tapped his ear. "The kid's taking part remotely, Ellie. You got your wish."

"Yes, John, but I didn't mean…" She shook her head. "Fine. Well done, you win. Come in, please."

They entered Lyne's flat and, at long last, the redness started. Still not as much as he'd expected, though. The other dog-murder crime scenes resembled an explosion at a blood bank. This one was just Lyne's body, mangled halfway off one of the leather chairs he'd so enjoyed, red mess limited to the pool around it.

"Um, still not much spatter, Choi. Going to look at the body now."

Ignoring Ellie, he went over to the chairs and sat down in the one Lyne wasn't using. His body was exactly where Hobson had last seen him: head and shoulders still sitting on the chair, legs hanging towards the ground. Those parts were unscathed, but between them was a bloody whirl of tearing. As if someone stuck a blender into his stomach, or held a dog's head tightly while it chewed and ripped at a single point.

There were intestines visible, Hobson saw the edge of a stomach, drying up but not yet starting to smell.

The scary black eyes were whiting out; skinny limbs made Lyne look skeletal after only a few hours dead. Second time in three days Hobson had come this close to fresh violence, but he wasn't getting used to it again yet.

The huge gash in Lyne's stomach was raw and frayed around the edges – thin, papery skin trailing off into blood. Hobson, as the external consultant, could feel the police in the room and Choi in his ear, all waiting for keen insight. All he could summon up was: "Fuck me."

"I'm alright, thanks John," Ellie came back first, "got anything else?"

"The arsehole must be bonding with his dog to get such a precise job here, after the last two bloody splatterfucks."

"Maybe it wasn't the dog? Maybe someone just wants us to think it is?"

"Maybe."

"Or Lyne was the killer and the dog turned on him?"

"Could be."

"Well, thanks for coming, John. You've been very useful."

"Oh, quiet down."

Hobson stood up and scanned across the room. Ended up gazing out of the huge window that made up one wall of Lyne's flat. In the mid-morning, the view was drab and grey, rather than the twinkling cityscape of last night. No romance anymore, he thought.

After the silence went on long enough, Choi piped up: "So, um, what's it like up there?"

"Not as messy as you'd think, Choi. Looks like our killer's been taking the dog to obedience classes, or doing the job himself with big knives."

"But how would they even get a dog up a building that cushy without someone noticing? I mean, I'm sitting down here looking at the entrance, the security on the door is huge, plus they might have cameras."

"You… raise a valid point." Hobson spoke slow, cogs whirring in his mind until he turned around. "Hey, Ellie, you turned the old CSI loose on this place yet? Any dog hairs in the lift or anything?"

"CSI?"

"Forensics. *Crusty Semen Inspectors.* Whatever you call them. The men with the microscopes."

"They've been and gone. We're talking to witnesses, but no-one seems to have seen anything."

"And Pete and Ric never moved from their house overnight?"

"Not according to the two officers watching it."

"I'm liking this, Ellie. It's like being a real cop."

"Get to the point, John, or I'll throw you out."

Hobson stood there, nodding for a few moments. He took another glance back at the window, and then finally made eye contact with Ellie. "Gotta go, Ellie. Sources to check out. But I think we're close. Let me know if the Semen People find anything."

"Yeah, okay." He was halfway out of the door already by the time she yelled after him: "John, I hope you're not hiding anything. Ex-husband or not, I won't tolerate you obstructing the police."

"Nope, of course not. Everything's great!"

He yelled that back to her just after pressing the button, and sighed as the lift doors closed. "Choi, you out there?"

"Yeah. What the hell just happened?"

"We're going back to Social Awesome. I gotta… check some records."

"It was Lyne, wasn't it? He's evil, just like we always knew?"

"No fuckin' comment."

"Guys! Hi!" Jacq said, waving as Angelina re-entered the Inspiration Gestation Station, Hobson just behind her. Angelina tried not to let her eyes widen at the sight of Jacq behind the reception desk, but couldn't quite manage it.

"Jacq, hi, weren't you…" Angelina took a few seconds to find the words, so of course, Hobson cut in.

"Dribbling, shouting and crying on a sofa like a crazy woman? And only yesterday, as well. You sure you should be in work?"

Jacq's smile stayed rooted beneath her tumble of hair, but the rest of her face wavered. "You were right, Mister Hobson, I heard you saying that nothing had really happened to me, so I shouldn't make too much of a fuss."

"Ah, well, you shouldn't take me too seriously, y'know, I say all kinds of shit. You wouldn't believe the amount of stuff I tell people to shove up their arse."

There was a silence as the two women let that sink in.

Angelina tried to summarise the situation. "What Hobson *meant* to say is: you shouldn't force yourself back to work just because he's rude."

"I'm fine," Jacq said, smiling still. "It's good to be back. I want people to take me seriously, you know? I don't want to be some precious flower who needs weeks off work to recover from a slight knock to the head. I mean, you're about twelve, you saw a lot more than me that night, and you're still going."

"I'm sixteen!" Angelina yelled out, as Hobson and Jacq burst into laughter.

"Anyway," Jacq said through the last of the snorts, "you guys want to go back up to Social Awesome?"

"Yeah, sign us in. Got to look at some stuff."

They filled out the visitor form and stepped into the flower-covered lift. Jacq kept eye contact and a firm smile until they were out of sight.

"Gotta say, I'm impressed with her." Hobson commented as they hummed upwards.

"You don't think she's a little not-okay underneath? Maybe she should let herself rest?"

"You are what you do, Choi. If she thinks she's up to coming in, no reason not to try. Gotta be better than Emily's sofa."

"I suppose."

Social Awesome was getting dusty. No-one had done a second of work there since Matt died, and Hobson couldn't imagine the death of the owner would encourage them. The desk chairs were all neatly pushed in, police forensics took Matt's body parts but refused to mop up the bloodstains. The smell was getting into the air now, even Hobson recoiled a little.

"Christ, you'd think the building would've cleaned up by now," Hobson grumbled to no-one in particular. "Do they ever want anyone to rent this office again?"

"So you think Social Awesome's finished?"

"Considering it was a scam to begin with, I can't see it surviving Lyne dying, no. That's why we're here."

She looked around the desks and stray papers. "Why?"

"To go through this stuff before they start emptying out the place. This is our chance to straighten out what's going on."

"I thought we'd already settled on Pete and Ric."

"We have. But we still gotta make sure we haven't missed anything, maybe find some clue." It was leg-work, it bored Hobson a little, but he wanted to close this case before the weekend and it was already Thursday lunchtime.

"Okay."

"Glad we settled that. So, one desk at a time, Choi. Let's try and get this over with in time for a sandwich."

An hour later, Hobson looked up from a file and yelled. "Okay, I think I'm nearly through. Can we run through who's still alive and make sure we're on the same page?"

His sidekick shrugged. "If you like."

"Okay, so: Emily Allen – blonde, bossy, executive complainer, fancied by Matt, William *and* Pete. Two of those guys now dead. Connection?"

"You think she killed Matt and William, so Pete is next?"

"Nah, not really. She doesn't like us, though."

"She's just *refined.* Maybe if you toned down the swearing."

"Shut the fuck up."

"Okay, my turn. Jacq Miller. Twee, quiet, lovable, probably not a serial killer."

"But, Choi, she does seem kind to animals. Maybe she bonded with the vicious dog and it turned her evil."

"Maybe. She does seem less pathetic than we suspected."

"Oh God, I was joking. Move on."

"Okay then… last woman in the group, Lettie Vole, Pete's sister. Angry, temperamental, swears almost as much as you. Does that make her a killer?"

"I dunno. Matt was her boyfriend and she seemed pretty upset when he died."

"Unless it was a cover."

"Unless it was a double-bluff."

"Really?"

"Nah, doubt it's her, but she might know something useful. Which brings us on to our likely real killer: Peter Vole. Lettie's brother, creepy, prone to unpleasant anger, needed more spanking as a child, in my expert fuckin' opinion."

"Thanks, Hobson."

"Any time. The question is, why? Jealousy over Emily, his sister, both? And why do Edward Lyne?"

"Throw us off the trail?"

"Maybe. Maybe he just likes being a serial killer. Desire for fame, y'know."

"And Pete's housemate Ric McCabe. You don't like him, do you?"

"No. Tedious, unfunny, tryhard prick. Stupid hair."

"I think he's fun."

"You're a teenage girl, you would. If he were still sixteen, his behaviour might be forgivable. But he isn't, so he should be next in line for that spanking."

"But you don't think he's the killer?"

"No, he's not got the balls. Might be covering Pete's tracks though."

Hobson leaned back and tossed his final file aside.

"Well, Choi, I've worked out that Pete expenses most of his lunches for no reason. What a tosser.

Let's beat him up regardless." Angelina didn't give him the courtesy of a response, so he dug harder. "You got anything?"

"Not much. Emily didn't lock the instant messenger logs on her computer, so I've got a load of Google Chat records showing her avoiding taking lunch at the same time as Pete *or* Matt."

"Print them out just in case."

Angelina blushed as she scrolled a bit further down. "Fair bit of, um, dodgy chats with William Lane too."

Hobson rose out of Pete's desk chair, circled around the bloodstains and leaned in over her shoulder, before bursting out laughing. It was so loud, her ears ached. "Brilliant. And disgusting. Don't let me catch you printing those out to take home."

Angelina closed the chat logs with a shudder and got up from Emily's computer. "Have we found anything useful yet?"

"No, it's all shit. I got one more big part to go, though: Lyne's private office."

In perfect sync, they looked over towards it. Door shut, it loomed in the corner like some grim cave, dragon inside ready to pounce.

"Want any help?"

"I'll be fine. If I remember rightly, he's got a ton of crap in there, so might take a while. Call Lettie Vole, okay? Get anything she knows about her brother's killing spree."

She nodded and reached for her mobile, while Hobson peeled off to start rooting through Lyne's effects. Then she realised she could save money by making the call on Social Awesome's line. It took a few rings before Lettie answered, sounding quiet and scared.

"Hello? Who is this, please?"

"Lettie, hi. You okay?"

"Angie? Why are you calling from that bloody office?"

"Oh, sorry, I'm just trying to save my minutes, you know..."

"For God's sake," Lettie said, as if normal conversation were beneath her.

"Look, do you have a minute to talk?"

"Yeah, I'd really like that. Come on over."

"I just meant over the..."

"No, I'd rather do it here if that's okay, things are a bit... Look, there's some stuff."

"Okay, okay. Your mum's house?" Angelina said, uneasy.

"Yeah."

"There as soon as I can. See you in a bit."

Angelina hung up and ran over to Lyne's office. Hobson was almost up to his knees in boxes of paper, shrouded in darkness thanks to closed blinds. It was enough to make him look scary. She stared for a moment.

"I did warn you," he said, looking up at last. "The dead bastard kept meticulous bloody records. Maybe we didn't have anything in common?"

"What?"

"Nothing. What did Lettie say?"

"I have to go meet her, sounds like she's got something to say. I didn't even have to mention Pete."

Hobson nodded, putting down his current plastic wallet. "Okay. Give me a sec to hide the good bits of Lyne's paperwork, then we'll get going."

"Um, she said just me, I don't think..."

"Choi, I know you want to take down London's underworld singlehanded, but you'll need to turn eighteen first."

"It's just Lettie! We're friends! You're not my Dad!"

"But your parents have spurned you, so I might as well be." He shoved a few sheets of paper down the back of a filing cabinet, and then started moving towards the lift. "Come on, Choi."

She stopped to think, but he looked over his shoulder. "Choi, you can't *lose* me, I already know where you're going."

Angelina sighed and started following after him, letting her feet scrape. This wouldn't even be anything important or exciting. Hobson was just being stupid.

THIRTEEN
ALL TOGETHER NOW

"Just wear the damn earpiece, Choi. This is my only damn condition, I'll let you go in if you use the mike."

"No!"

They were standing in the small road turning leading into the square, after lunch on a blowy winter Thursday. Only two or three minutes' walk away was the Vole family home.

Pedestrians were side-glancing at their argument – a few recognised them and asked about the case. All were shooed away, but refused to disappear. Instead, they hovered at the top end of the road and watched.

Hobson nearly gave them a redirection they'd never forget, but Choi stopped him. It would spread all over Twitter and be bad for business, she said. So he stayed quiet, thinking about the people he'd like to spread all over Twitter.

Not to mention, Choi was providing plenty of heated debate already: "I didn't want you to come in the first place! I'll be fine; I'll just tell you what she says."

"Come on, look, it might be dangerous. Stick this in your ear, or I'll go to the meeting instead. Maybe tell Lettie you're locked in a sandwich shop toilet with the exploding shits."

"She wouldn't talk to you. She only wants to talk to me."

"I'm sure I could trick the tip out of her, but wouldn't it be better if you wore this black box and behaved yourself, eh?"

There was a silent spell, while Choi glared at him. Not giving an inch, he just held out his hand with the black box and accessories. Slowly, she arranged the wires around herself, clipped the mike inside her blouse, screwed the earpiece into place and gave one last evil look. He didn't react. Eventually, she turned into the square to knock on Lettie's door.

Sighing with relief, Hobson leaned against the wall, tuning his own earpiece in. Once he looked up from adjusting the dial, he realised a couple of his fans had crept closer.

Well, no pressure to be polite now she'd gone.

"Okay, show's over." He pointed back towards the busy main road. "Fuck off and get a real job. Some of us are trying to do something useful, rather than read about it on Twitter."

As she crossed the square to Lettie's house, Angelina did her utmost to look cool, calm and collected.

She mounted the pavement without tripping up, avoided the foliage from the central garden, and noticed residents appearing at windows as she passed. Nonetheless, she kept on track.

Until she was facing the Vole house, wavering over whether to knock on the main door or the lower entrance into the basement. Was she meant to be bypassing Lettie's mum? Paralysed at the bottom of the steps, she felt oh-so-conscious of how this looked to Hobson and everyone else.

The front door swung open and there Violet Vole stood.

"Angie! You okay? Come on!"

Not hiding her relief, Angelina dashed up the steps until she reached Lettie. Now they were close, Angelina saw her pale skin, even more starkly white next to the red hair, and bloody, tired eyes.

"I'm fine. Are you alright? You sounded weird on the phone."

"I'm fine too. Come in." Lettie gestured behind her. "God knows who's watching out there."

Not reassured by her paranoia, Angelina slipped through the door into their hallway. It slammed hard behind her. The upstairs entrance hall of the Vole house was musty, old and felt thoroughly lived in. Family photos jostled for space with shoes, coats, keys and bags, yet it didn't feel cluttered or messy, just *used.*

Stairs spilled away up and down, the walls were a faded green colour. Indoors, with no windows here and all the lights off, it felt like a haunted house.

"So, um, you said you wanted to talk. What's up?"

"Yeah, do you want to sit down?" Lettie gestured to the first door on their left, and as expected, it was a living room. More hefty wooden furniture, photos and assorted ornaments, nice-looking sofas and huge TV.

No sign of anyone else in the house, dull winter light streaming into the room. Everything looked washed out, complimenting Lettie's mood.

Angelina sat on the sofa and remembered how she'd rehearsed this.

"So, I guess you heard what happened to Edward Lyne by now?" she began, talking fast.

"Yeah, I did, I'm, um…" Lettie sat opposite Angelina, squinting for a second, then gestured towards her own ears. "What's that, headphones?"

"No, this is, um, it's a microphone thing."

"So Hobson's listening to every word we're saying?"

"Yeah. Um. Sorry, he made me do it."

"Okay. Take them out, turn them off, whatever the fuck. Cut him off."

All of a sudden, she wanted to preserve the earpiece badly. "Are you sure? It might help if he knows…"

Hobson's voice concurred. "Choi, listen, this is fuckin' dodgy, don't do it."

She paused, gulped, nodded, and yanked the recording device off. Untangled all the wires, pulled the black box from her pocket and dropped it on the glass coffee table in front of her with a clunk. After a last hopeful look at Lettie, she reached out a hand and turned the dial at the end, until the small green light clicked off.

"Okay. Let's talk."

Hobson shouted *"Fuck!"* so loud, the rubberneckers dashed out of cover to see if something good had happened. He flicked them a swift middle finger, then moved up the small road to get the Vole house in sight.

Christ. How long should he give it before kicking the door in?

"So, um, you said you know Lyne is dead?"

After a minute of silent staring at the radio box, Angelina wanted the conversation to start up again.

"Yeah, I know. I saw. I… yeah."

"And I guess you're pretty happy? Since last time I saw you, you were all hatey hatey rage rage?"

"Yeah, shit, you think many people know about that?"

"Depends if you told them, I guess. Why?"

Lettie still focused her vague eyes on the mess of tangled wires. "Because I, um, killed him. Edward Lyne. After I heard the police just let him go. I went in there and hacked him up and hoped people would think it was the dog guy."

Angelina's hand twitched. God. What would Hobson do now?

"Oh *fuck*."

"Fuck. Yeah." Lettie didn't sound angry, just sad. "It didn't even feel good."

"I guess it wouldn't, I…" Angelina sank back into her chair, wondering if there was some way to get Hobson in here. "So you… I mean, all that stuff Hobson described to me earlier, ripping open his entire stomach, you did… with knives?"

"Yeah. It isn't much like cutting a turkey."

"No?"

"No. Messier. Parts slide around and beat at you. Like you've stuck your hand into a soft working engine."

"Did he fight back?"

"He let me in, I don't think he expected… it was too late by the time he could've done something, he just gave up. And then there was blood everywhere." Lettie leaned forward, her tangled mess of red hair fell over her eyes. The light from the window kept greying her out.

"And he didn't say anything?"

"He told me he had nothing to do with William and Matt dying. Seemed pretty fucking smug about that. I still think he was lying."

Lettie looked around and grabbed a cushion, hugging it against her body and burying her face. It was hard enough to understand her already.

Eventually, she tilted her eyes upwards to meet Angelina's. "Tell me he did it, Angie."

"What?"

"Tell me it was him and I didn't kill a guy for nothing."

"Well, everyone knew he was a bastard. He was conning people, Hobson says there's dodgy stuff in his paperwork, he looked like the grim reaper's accountant. I'm sure there's reasons he deserved to die, y'know?"

Lettie was shaking even with the cushion now. "But he didn't do it? He didn't kill Matt?"

"No, I don't… I mean, Hobson doesn't seem to think so."

Lettie choked up, leaned her head into her hand for a while, and finally reared up. Drew her arm back and hurled the cushion across the room. It skimmed along the shelf above the TV, sending a few china figurines smashing to the floor. She crumpled back up in the chair and started crying.

But even then, she wasn't finished. "Who was it, then?"

"Lettie, I don't think you need to…"

She unfurled in a flash, whole face red and damp, breathing heavy, and roared into Angelina's face: *"Tell me now!"* Then, smirking: "Unless you still haven't fucking worked it out."

"No, I mean, we're not *totally* sure, but Hobson seems to suspect, um." Angelina swallowed and said:

"Pete. Your brother. He seems to be pretty, um, he's been acting weird."

"God. So he's killing people as well? We're quite the fucking family."

"Yeah."

"I told Pete I killed Lyne, as well. I called him. He said not to tell anyone and he'd be over soon."

Angelina's eyes flew wide at that, not to mention the sound of a car outside. "Here? He's coming here? Right now?"

"Yeah. Guess that means you and your boss can get us both packaged up for the cops."

"No, I mean, you were trying to help, I'm sure Hobson wouldn't…"

"You reckon?"

Their eyes flicked up towards the bay windows onto the street. Before either could get up, there was a crash and a few shouts. Angelina couldn't understand all of it, but she heard her own surname and a few swearwords.

Both Lettie and Angelina dashed over to the window.

A black car rumbled up behind him. It was a small vehicle, but impressive still, consisting mostly of front seats and a decent sized boot.

More interesting, though, was the face behind the wheel. Pete Vole stared back at Hobson, then drove steadily into the square, aiming for the house. Technically, this *was* his family home, the man had every right to be here.

Still, it was too much of a coincidence and Hobson was twitchy as hell.

Before Vole even closed the car door, his ginger rat-faced head looked up to see Hobson's huge frame bearing down on him. Pete wasn't a big man, but there was muscle underneath the coat, Hobson saw. And no shirt, just a stained hoodie, bags under the eyes. Still, he was defensive, rather than cowering.

Hobson stopped arm's length from Pete and nodded. "Mister Vole. Visiting the family?"

"Yes. Why, does that prove I'm mental?"

"Your sister's busy talking to my assistant. Mind waiting out here until they've finished?"

Pete's eyes widened, he didn't even keep talking, just turned and raced up the steps to the front door as if his car was about to explode. Come to think of it, the thing was making a weird huffing noise, but Hobson didn't have time to investigate that right now.

He paced up the stone steps himself, reached out and locked his right arm around Pete's neck from behind. "So, Pete – mind if I call you Pete – why don't you want your sister talking to Choi?"

"I… it's…"

Hobson squeezed tighter. "She know something about you? You call her to confess killing her boyfriend with your doggy? That it?"

"No… I mean…"

The door to the Vole house swung open. There, at the top of the steps, stood Lettie and Choi, both alive and well. Not injured anyway – the Vole girl looked one sad song away from self-harm.

"What's happening? Pete?" She sounded terrified. "What's…"

"Lettie," he gasped through Hobson's grip, "don't say anything, it's fine!"

"Ah, for fuck's sake, Vole, give it up." Hobson pulled Pete around and looked him straight in the eye.

"You killed them all. You left the dog at home for Lyne because it was too conspicuous. Admit it before your sister blows her own brains out."

Pete didn't reply, just breathed faster. Choi stood there above them all, mouth opening and closing like a confused fish. People emerged from their houses around the square.

"No, you don't *understand*," Lettie finally sobbed out, loud enough for everyone to hear, "it was…"

Pete shoved Hobson with one hand, and this guy really was unexpectedly strong. He sent the bigger detective staggering down to the pavement.

Before Hobson could recover his footing, Pete stormed the front door and forced the two women back inside the house. Choi didn't seem happy about it, but he grabbed hold of her arm and yanked. Hobson thought he heard her yelling his name just before the door slammed, lock clicked into place. Looked like one hell of a thick door, too.

Alone in the square, staring up at that townhouse, Hobson wondered whether the downstairs basement door was easier to smash open. There was a click from Pete's car and he turned around, losing his train of thought. Vole must have one of those remote controls for his boot door. As it popped open, the light breathing noise from earlier became much louder.

The back trunk door of the car jerked up from its light sitting position, and the grey, long body jumped out. It growled and stalked towards him. Yalin Makozmo's fighting animal didn't seem happy about travelling in the back compartment of a small car. The claws and teeth were huge, the eyes staring.

The rumours were true: this dog was the size of a jungle predator. All sharp edges and blood-matted fur. Well, Hobson thought, after all this time, he was going to fight a wolf after all. He hoped they appreciated it on Twitter.

It gave one sharp bark, before launching itself towards him.

FOURTEEN
CRAZY LIKE A WOLF

As the door crashed shut, Angelina snatched at it, but Pete caught her around the waist and almost threw her backwards. She hit him in the shoulder with a flailing arm, but still ended up back in the hallway.

She and Lettie exchanged wide eyes, and then turned to Pete.

"Pete," Lettie started, "what're you doing?"

"Did you tell *her*?" Pete indicated Angelina. "About… about him?"

"Yeah, sorry, I just… had to talk to someone."

"You were supposed to wait for me!"

"You weren't here!"

"For fuck's sake, couldn't you…"

All that bickering was cut off by the loud roar of a dog barking outside, and Angelina found her voice. "Oh God, is that the wolf?"

Pete rolled his eyes. "It's not a wolf, it's a wolf*hound*. A huge one, but still, don't be so hysterical."

"Is it about to eat Hobson?"

"That's what I'm hoping for."

"Then why shouldn't I be *fucking hysterical?*"

Angelina reached for the front door, grasping and clawing for the locks. Once again, Pete kept her back without even needing two hands.

"Into the living room," he beckoned. "Where we can see what's happening out there."

Without much hope of escape, Angelina followed his orders.

Hobson hadn't fought many animals in his time. Dog, wolf, whichever this was, it scared him. He backed away down the pavement as it dribbled and stalked away from the car.

Panicking, he tried a massive slap towards it, in case it instinctively backed off. Remembering Matt Michaelson's dissected arm didn't give him much hope, but maybe it needed a firm hand.

His blow swept through the air, missing the dog's head, and the black shape took both a swipe *and* a bite at it, baring hundreds of sharp teeth. It had red, bloody eyes with thin slits for pupils, just like wolves on TV, howling as well as barking. Its grey fur was either naturally red-tinted or still blood-stained because Pete hadn't bothered washing it.

The dog shook its head with another growl, taking a few paces back as Hobson recoiled. Its swipe hadn't reached his arm, but raked through his coat, which cost him a whole case worth of wages. Hobson took a kick at the dog's head with his heavy boot. Let's see the little fuck walk this off.

The foot glanced off its ear, leaving his leg open for the jaws. The black suit trousers provided some cover, but nowhere near enough. He roared a medley of horrible swearing, sinking down to one knee trying to pull it away. Blood trickled down his shin, as the creature went after his lower leg like it was a bone.

The residents of the square stayed close to their front doors, keeping their mobile phone cameras trained on Hobson and his dogfight. Hopefully one of them had the decency to call the police.

Pete pulled the curtains wide to see the fight, without stepping too near the window. The other two were side-by-side on the sofa as he'd instructed.

Lettie was beginning to glare at her brother with familiar fury. He looked back whenever they made a sudden movement, but no-one said anything until there was a roar from Hobson outside. Didn't sound like the fight was going well, so Angelina wouldn't livetweet it.

Instead, she unfurled to her feet, and Pete took his eyes from the window to say "Sit down."

"No. So it was you all along?"

"Maybe."

"That's *the* dog out there, isn't it? The one that killed Yalin Makozmo, William and Matt. You were keeping it somewhere."

"Sit down, *please*." His teeth gritted, fist clenching. Maybe he *would* punch her, Angelina thought, until Lettie stood up too, placing herself in front of Angelina.

"Pete. Enough, okay? Let's just both go outside, tell them what happened and take our chances."

"Don't be so fucking stupid, Lettie."

"I'm the fucking stupid one?" Lettie exploded. "You just set the murder weapon on a fucking detective in fucking broad fucking daylight!"

"Look, I thought maybe it would kill him, then the police would take it out, then maybe..."

"Maybe what? A dozen people saw it come out of your car! It's over, okay? We'll do this together."

"No. We're not both going to prison for this."

"What happened anyway?"

Angelina kept level eyes with Pete as she asked the question. May as well try and get some information out of him. She read the introduction to that A Level Psychology textbook, she was almost prepared to negotiate with someone properly crazy.

Hobson dragged himself along the pavement, jabbing at the dog with his good foot. Fuck. The injured leg picked up a head of steam as it bled, leaving a smeared trail behind. The dog growled itself into a frenzy, chasing him and clawing for the wound.

His trousers were fucked, leg didn't look good either.

It stopped following him along, grazing at the injury. Hobson stared its red eyes down, at the same level as his now. Listened to the heavy rasp of its breathing and hoped it would go bother someone else.

A moment later, it lunged for his torso and head.

Pete looked like he might ignore her question or punch her for a moment, but at last, he shrugged.

"I'd just had a huge argument with William over Emily, he told me she thought I was sad and creepy. I went to sulk in the garden, kinda a habit I'd gotten into, and that's when I saw it."

Angelina didn't need to ask what he meant.

"The dog already had blood on its muzzle anyway. So I whacked it around with sticks, got it good and angry, then managed to shove it at William. And while it was ripping him up, I locked the door and kicked the thing through from outside."

"And why Matt?"

"I heard about his meet-up with these two, and he might've worked it out. He'd heard stuff from Emily, they sat next to each other."

"Wait!" Lettie stepped so close to Pete, she was breathing into his mouth. "You killed my boyfriend because he *might've worked it out*? Are you absolutely crazy?"

"Well, I couldn't just let him… I mean, I didn't…"

"And after all that, you did this shit anyway?"

"Oh, come on Lettie. Hobson definitely knew, this was the last chance. If he survived, he'd make sure I went down."

Angelina spoke up. "And I wouldn't?"

"You're just a kid. I was going to give you this chance to keep quiet."

"She won't," Lettie said, without even checking with Angelina, "and neither will I. What're you going to do now, Pete? Kill us both?"

He didn't reply, just stared over at the sharp edges of the ceramic figures Lettie smashed earlier. Angelina didn't like that look in his eyes.

Ever headbutted a dog?

Hobson wouldn't normally, but with both his hands clasped around his own bleeding shin and a pair of stinking jaws coming fast for his nose, there wasn't much choice. Eyes closed and fists clenched, he rolled his head forward as hard as he could. The beast's teeth scraped across his forehead, doggy legs flapped around its body as it bounced away.

His eyes opened again, only to wince back shut as blood poured from a gaping hole in his brow. Hobson tried to rub them clear but only made his fingers sticky, crawling up the pavement as his trailing leg roared at him to stop.

A couple of the thing's teeth were broken but the rest of it still worked fine. It reared up for another go, but Hobson could only see a prowling outline. He could hear a little girl screaming and didn't know whether it was real.

He was going to die, wasn't he? Bleed out on the pavement because of some stupid yuppies and their rabid puppy.

A strange defiant acceptance came over him. His hand slacked and fell open. There were sirens in the distance. Ellie said *John*, but it wasn't real. He knew that, because a second later, another female voice, deeper and older, said "Mister Hobson?"

The dog looked up, growling. Hobson tried to do the same, then fell back down again.

"Lettie, grab her!"

Pete went for the broken china, while Lettie and Angelina stood dead still. No one grabbed anybody. Couldn't look away from Pete scrabbling around on the carpet.

His hand closed around a broken porcelain fairy, vicious spike sticking upwards where her skirt should be. Pete jerked back up to face them, eyes wide. Lettie shook her head at him.

"Put the thing down, Pete," she said. "Mum'll be pissed off enough that I broke it without you getting blood all up it."

"Lettie, if we don't stop them we'll never…"

"Pete, I don't know if you were always this crazy, but we're screwed either way. You can't save me or yourself by stabbing Angie. Even if she died and the wolf ate Hobson, we'd still be locked up."

She held her hand out to him, unable to stop it shaking. Angelina's entire shoulders were trembling even more.

"Now give me the stupid fucking fairy-spike and let's get this over with."

There were definitely sirens outside now. Angelina heard Hobson roaring, another burst of dog noises. She bit back the urge to rush to the window.

Pete stood there, twitching all over. The jagged china in his hand moved, and Angelina thought he'd shove it into Lettie's gut. Instead, he reached out to place it in her outstretched palm.

Until a woman's voice outside, gruff, posh-accented and loud, said "Mister Hobson?"

The dog growled, as the two Vole siblings turned to the front of the house and shouted: *"Mum?"*

They both bundled into the hallway and started ripping at the front door. Unsure what else to do, Angelina hurried along behind them.

By the time she made it out to the front step, Pete had thrown himself down to street level and torn across the square.

Mrs Vole was returning from the big shopping centre down the road, swatting at the vicious dog with an overloaded TK Maxx bag. For a moment, it played along, batting at the swinging plastic with a huge spiked paw. Before Angelina could breathe easy, it got bored and ripped the whole thing open with a swipe.

The garish clothes dropped out, covering its head and sending it back into a rage. Mrs Vole let out a scream that made Angelina's ears hurt. Just as the dog was ready to tear into her, it heard footsteps behind and turned to see Pete.

After all the time locked up, that animal *hated* him. Losing interest in Mrs Vole, it let out a savage noise and sprang forward immediately, taking a slash at Pete's midriff and tearing into his coat and stinking hoodie.

He backed up to get away, just about making enough distance to avoid a gutting. Lettie pulled their Mum back, as Pete tripped over the kerb and lost his footing, falling to one knee. Sensing easy victory, the bloody, tangled dog barked roughly and slashed forward, claws out.

If Pete hadn't been holding that spear of broken china, it would've been the end of his head. Instead, he impaled the black shaggy shape hard through the neck as it raked its claws across his cheek. The two of them collapsed onto the road, dog's blood running out over Pete's face and mingling with his own.

As they both fell still, Angelina's eyes zipped from there to the pavement outside the house, where Hobson was still collapsed in a pile. The emergency services were pulling up in the square, arriving in time to be no help at all. Angelina let out an irritated huff before kneeling down next to her boss. She made sure not to look at the blood smeared across his face and trailing out from his leg.

"Hobson! Hey!" No response. "You alright? Hobson?"

She shook one huge shoulder with both hands. "Hobson?"

He focused his eyes on her long enough to seem exasperated, before the paramedics shoved her aside.

They worked on him, more blood came out. Angelina felt squeamish again, so tried to get back into earshot of the Vole family as they spoke to Ellie. The police detective kept looking over towards Hobson.

Pete sat on the pavement, a large bandage over the cut on his face, not looking much like a crazed serial killer. A paramedic hovered nearby, worried expression on her face, but Ellie wasn't letting him go for medical attention yet.

"So, this is the dog that killed all those people?" She gestured down towards the huge canine body on the floor. Even dead, it was terrifying, Angelina thought, flopped down with tongue hanging out. It might be bigger than she was.

"Yeah," Pete said. Lettie almost opened her mouth too, before he cut her off: "So, it was me, okay? I killed them *all*. I didn't use the dog on the last kill because it was too conspicuous."

Ellie nodded. "Okay. Peter, you'll be coming with us after you've had treatment for that cut. You may want to wait until you have a lawyer present before you say any more."

"No, look…" Lettie said.

"Lettie," Pete shouted her down. She looked ready to yell over him, until Mrs Vole spun on her feet and fainted. She came close to squashing the dog corpse as she fell, and she wasn't a small lady, it might've burst like a furry blood-balloon. Angelina would have *hurled.*

Instead, she thudded to the pavement with a crack, paramedics hurried over to attend her. Ellie waved a few officers around to supervise Pete during his stitches, and told Angelina and Lettie not to go anywhere.

At last, Ellie let herself check on Hobson. Only Angelina and Lettie left standing outside the Vole house, a strange quiet between them. No one in a high-vis vest nearby, so Angelina felt free to ask: "Well, um, I guess you're not going to prison."

"I suppose not. But part of me feels I should just confess to killing Lyne. I mean, my fucking brother came clean, and he's off the hook mental."

"Maybe he's trying to do some good by taking the blame."

"He'll regret that when I kill again."

"That was a joke, right?"

Lettie gave a wry, mirthless smile. "Yeah."

"Good." Angelina jabbed at the ground with her toe. "Good, good."

Hobson wasn't paying attention to much. He got the impression he'd solved another case, which was satisfying. Always good to cross one off the list. Fucking hell, he was a genius.

The mobile doctoring men were patching up his leg, so he probably wouldn't die today either. Couldn't walk, move or feel anything, but wasn't complaining. Nice not to worry.

He could just lie back and pretend everything was okay again.

A second later, Ellie knelt down beside him, put her hand on his arm, said "John," and the trick was complete.

FIFTEEN
A LONG WEEKEND

On Friday morning, Hobson woke up in his flat and looked around the place. Nothing was happening. He made a point of keeping his home tidy, no casual drinking or ordering takeaway – all part of staying clean. He was a force of nature, trapped in a deliberately boring life.

He dragged himself into his tedious kitchen and began making a green smoothie. The wounded leg still hurt like hell, even with the stitches and painkillers, so he dropped another couple of pills, even though he couldn't remember when he'd taken the last dose. He wouldn't end up using a cane, would he? Hobson may have retired from the all-action life, but that didn't mean he wanted to be a cripple.

As he sipped the horrible veg-goo, he wondered what to do now. Ellie accompanied him to the hospital, but hadn't hung around long. Once the docs confirmed he wouldn't lose the leg, just needed stitches and injections against animal diseases, she'd patted him on the head and left to start processing Pete Vole.

Maybe he'd call Choi, he thought, before shaking his head. She's about seven years old and his work experience girl, *not* a friend. Hobson turned to his last resort: putting the TV on.

Angelina always enjoyed visiting her friend Zoë's house, treating it as a fun exercise in the unfamiliar. Zoë's parents were chatty and messy, their house a tip, cardboard boxes spilling clutter everywhere. Angelina's Mum would faint at the sight of it, which made hiding from her here all the more satisfying.

They made it to Zoë's room with a takeaway pizza and talked work experiences, as shelves of coloured book series creaked around them.

"How's it going, Angelina? Is it exciting working for a detective? I bet it's pretty exciting. I saw you guys working on that dog murder on the TV."

"Well, yeah, it was pretty amazing at times, I saw loads of… I mean… it was cool, but you know, people died. Some of them I knew, too, that was sad."

"And how about being on the news?"

"That was a bit… I dunno, they wouldn't leave us alone. It's not as fun as it looks," she said, trying to crack a smile. "My parents aren't super-keen on me working there, but hopefully I'll get to finish it out."

"Oh, right," said Zoë.

"How's yours?" Angelina said.

"Oh, it's been quite interesting, actually."

"Yes?"

"Yeah! I learnt to do a VLOOKUP on Excel and generated a load of spreadsheets for the MD and she said I'm just the sort of enterprising young woman who could go far and she's the most successful woman ever in the company and she said to call me if I ever…"

Angelina tuned out.

"Evening, Tony."

"John. You look like shit."

Hobson limped around the table and dragged the chair out, inch by scraping inch, before levering himself into place for an arse-drop. When it came, Tony almost jumped out of his seat, an amusing physical jerk from one so skinny.

"Jesus," he said on recovery. "So, this is why you dragged me out to your neighbourhood."

"Yeah. Sorry, Tony. No long commutes right now."

"Fucking good footage of your dogfight on the telly, though."

"Yeah?"

"Fuck yeah. Makes you look like a total superhero."

"Really? Even though I nearly died and had to be rescued by a chubby housewife?"

"Maybe not a *total* superhero, but y'know." Tony shrugged. "No publicity is bad publicity, right?"

"So my assistant tells me. Not sure I'm agreeing, though."

"This the Asian girl?"

"Yeah, Choi." Hobson said. "She's got one of her two weeks left to finish me off."

"Finish you off? John, she's made you a star!" Tony said, lunging forward to gesticulate into Hobson's face. "Have you checked your office email in the last two days?"

"I've been avoiding them."

"Do it, man. Two of my friends asked if I could fast-track their cases 'cause we're mates. I'm telling you, Johnny, you're like the Simon Cowell of crime."

"Tony, I know the Simon Cowell of crime and he ain't me. And don't call me *Johnny*."

Tony flopped back in his chair to shake his head at Hobson. The rest of the pub kept going around them, clattering, drinking and chatting. Even this quiet shithole lit up on a Saturday night – it was awful.

"What's your problem, John? You solved the case, you're not dead, you're crime-fighting flavour of the month – it's all good, innit?"

"Firstly, I'm meant to be staying away from violent crime, I don't need it phoning me up. Secondly, I won't be getting shit from that case because the client got dogged to death."

"Ah, that's some balls. Didn't he leave you anything in his will or nothing?"

"No, he just..." Hobson sat straight upright, drawing stranger looks from Tony. "Wait."

"What?"

"Just remembered, he did leave me something. We might be alright after all." Hobson grinned to himself for a few seconds, then looked up at Tony. "Now hurry up and get me a drink, I'm fuckin' disabled over here."

After some wheedling and begging, Angelina negotiated an overnight stay at her friend's house. Wouldn't last forever though. Zoë had ballet class for three hours the next morning, and Angelina couldn't follow her there.

She tried, but Zoë got weird about it after a few minutes. Even the library could only kill a couple more hours. So she went home at lunchtime on Saturday, as the wind whipped harder outside.

Could she make it up to her loft without confrontation? Angelina got one foot on the bottom stair before her Mum emerged from the kitchen. Eyes staring as ever, usual look of recent crying around her face.

"Hi, Mum." Another stupid impotent wave – must stop doing that.

"Angelina. Are you… are you okay?"

"Yeah. I was fine. You saw on the news? Never in any danger."

"Except when you were in the house with the murderer for twenty minutes."

"That doesn't count."

"Why not?"

"Because…" Angelina dropped to the ground floor, groaning. "Because it doesn't, okay Mum?"

"Are you going back there on Monday?" She spoke and at a measured, careful pace, determined not to lose her temper.

"Hope so, as long as Hobson's okay. Are you going to try and stop me?"

"No."

"Right. Look, I'm sorry I threatened you and stuff, okay? That was… that wasn't good of me."

"No, look," tears again, "I know I get worked up sometimes, but it is only because I worry. There is real danger too, I don't think I'm being hysterical."

"I know."

"If this is really what you want, okay, but can you at least try and stick to less dangerous cases?"

"I suppose so."

"Okay."

"Okay."

They paused for a while, then Angelina instigated a hug. Her observations of past conversations suggested that would bring proceedings to a close. Sure enough, she was soon on her way back upstairs.

Maybe Angelina was biased, but her apology had been way better than her Mum's. More sincere too.

As she flopped backwards onto the bed in her personal loft conversion, Angelina wondered if it was time to move on. If her real parents would understand her more. If Hobson was the right guy to help her find them.

She'd have to get her feet properly under the table first.

Hobson obtained access to the Inspiration Gestation Station by calling the building owner until he agreed to open the building up on a Sunday just to end the phone calls. After taking a huge dose of painkillers to stop his leg complaining too much, he jumped on the train over there.

Tell the truth, he *could* have met Tony at a more mutually convenient pub last night. Still, what use is a horrific injury if it doesn't get favours out of your friends?

He rolled up outside the IGS and looked around. He'd been told someone would meet him to open the doors. Sure enough, Jacq ran up from the street behind him a minute later, breathless and falling over herself to get there on schedule.

"Mister Hobson! Sorry! Running late! My local Overground was closed!"

"Building owner got you out of bed? Sorry 'bout that, just want to take a look at something."

"Oh, it's no trouble, Mister Hobson."

"Just Hobson, c'mon."

Jacq shrugged as she rooted in her bag for the building key. "Calling people by surnames just seems strange to me," she said, "sorry about that."

"Stop apologising, too. So you're still alright? Not gone back to crying on a sofa?"

"No sir. No point in that, I told you. Don't want people to think I'm silly."

"Good girl. Like your spirit."

She might've blushed, hard to tell against her already-flushed cheeks. "Thanks, Mister Hobson."

Jacq pulled the key out, opened the front door and they stepped into the darkened reception. Hobson was hit by a flashback to last week's bloody night when Matt died, but shook it off with a twitch.

The lights flickered on, and Jacq dashed behind her reception desk, dropping her massive bag on top of it. Immediately, she seemed more comfortable. "Did you want me to turn the lift on for you, Mister Hobson?"

"No worries thanks, I'll take the stairs. Gotta size the place up, see if there's any furniture worth saving."

"What do you mean?"

"I'm moving in, Jacq. Taking over the old Social Awesome office."

"I thought you hated it here?"

"I do. But it's much bigger. Also negotiated the chief twat of the building down way low, 'cause I don't care about working in a bloody murder site. Choi might not like it, I suppose, but she can man up."

"Aha. Very clever."

"Also, most of the pricks phoning offering me jobs live in this area. Gotta move with the times, Ms Miller. Now, if I give you some money, will you run out and get us both Subways?" He paused. "Or is that demeaning?"

"No, I like Subway, and it's better than just waiting around here." She grinned.

"Good. Bring it up when you're back."

Jacq seized her bag and ran round the desk to pluck the money from his hand. Within seconds, she locked the door behind her again. Another quick smile before she dashed down the pathway. Hobson shook his head, unused to dealing with this kind of cheer.

Putting it out of his mind for now, he barged through the door to storm the stairs. There was another reason he'd obtained this office: Edward Lyne had reams of interesting paperwork still in his filing cabinets. Hobson wanted all of it; there were leads to follow up, and the building manager had agreed to turn a blind eye for a while.

Most crucial of all was a large folder labelled *JOHN HOBSON*. He'd glimpsed it the other day when he and Choi had searched the place. Looked like a full account of his life to date, covering incidents that even the police shouldn't know about. He wasn't letting Lyne's personal effects out of his sight until he'd solved that mystery.

HOBSON & CHOI
WILL RETURN
IN

CASE TWO:
RUSH JOBS

BONUS STORY

THE LEFT HAND IS ALWAYS RIGHT

In the cheap pubs, the old men sat, nursing their pints and muttering to themselves. Anna could see why they ended up here – obviously didn't have the money to plant themselves in a trendy gastropub all day.

A few were clearly here with mates, but others merely permanent items of the pub's sticky furniture. The Left Hand wasn't even a regular venue for Anna, just too horrible, but she still recognised some of them. Big old men, small ones, real ale or cheap lager, some sticking to the bar, others sharing their table with a free newspaper they'd read six times.

Once she got chatting to her friends, maybe knocked back a couple of drinks, Anna could ignore them. The dark mutterings under their breath, the way their eyes sometimes flicked up to her. But there was a problem with her strategy. She was stuck alone at a table in the back half of the pub, nice and visible in the middle, nursing a drink and getting twitchy.

All Chloe's fault. The only reason she ever came to this rathole was because it was near Chloe's house and she couldn't always persuade her friend not to be bone idle. Most times, Chloe at least did Anna the favour of turning up on time, after making her haul her arse over from Wood Green.

But she wasn't here, and showed no sign of arriving. Messages went unanswered, one phone call went straight to voicemail. Probably still at work or asleep on the sofa.

It was Tuesday night, so the old men were really swarming. Or perhaps there weren't enough young people to dilute them.

Anna glanced up from her mobile and took another tiny sip of her wine, nursing it until Chloe arrived to buy her an apology drink. As she raised her eyes to get the glass, they panned around the room. At least two of the scary guys were staring at her. From under their hats, above their beards, inside their red faces.

Sitting in a pub drinking alone, normally she'd hope some arsehole wouldn't clumsily try to get in her pants. Right now, the arrival of someone age-appropriate and not-terrifying appealed, even if they were a dickbag. Or maybe she'd change her mind once the situation came up.

No sign of any pricks, so she'd never know. Just the two staring old men. Anna glanced back at her mobile, just because. Maybe there would be an interesting post on Facebook. It had to happen eventually.

She kept looking up at the two of them, wary like prey in the jungle, waiting for either to make a move.

Nothing stirred. Seemed still. Kept without motion.

But they probably thought her constant checking up on them was weird.

Still no word from Chloe.

As she jerked up to take another look, there was a gentle clunk behind her.

Anna wasn't sitting with her back against the wall, of course. She took a table with space behind it specially to avoid getting trapped, then didn't keep an eye on the weak spot until now, rolling around to see an entirely new muttering, decrepit male.

She'd half-seen him when sitting down, then directed all her attention at the rest of the pub where the majority nested.

This guy was wearing a ratty shirt, browning around the edges, as if left in a puddle for too long. The jeans were going the same way, trapped forever in place due to circumstances. He was in a wheelchair, not one of those electric mobility scooters, but a metal frame, propelled by arm strength alone. His hair was straggly and thinning, eyes sunken. Fingers gripped his drink as tight as possible.

Not as old as the rest, early forties maybe, but just as ruined. Maybe more so, serious scarring around his face.

"Sorry, ma'am," he said, after it became clear she wasn't going to make a sound. "Are you waiting for someone?"

"Yes," Anna replied, keen to send him on his way. "My friend. She's late."

"Ah, well, that's rude isn't it?"

He was pushing against the walls of her innate Britishness. She could say *Look, go away,* but that would to be rude. Not to mention he was disabled, so she could probably beat him up if need be. He wasn't too creepily old, looked like he might even have been attractive before he turned to ravaged alcoholism.

Not to mention, she'd seen him and then disregarded him as a non-worthwhile non-threat, probably because he was in a wheelchair. So she was probably a terrible person.

Working through that maelstrom of guilt, she let it go for now. At least he might pass the time.

"I suppose so."

"Definitely," he said, eyes sparking up a little as he realised she wasn't telling him to fuck off and die. "I'm Danny."

"Hi, I'm Chloe," Anna nodded. That'd teach the cow for being late.

"Hi Chloe. So, how are you?"

"I'm fine. Bit tired."

Terribly rude of her not to ask after his welfare, but she couldn't bring herself to do it. Add it to the guilt list. Where the fuck was Chloe?

He chuckled.

"You looked terrified, don't worry. I'm not some lunatic."

"Sorry," Anna said, still unable to stop her muscles tensing.

"Ah, Chloe, it's okay. Everyone looks at me like that. Honestly, if I met me before I was like this, I'd do the same *Oh-God-please-just-disappear* eyes I'm getting from you."

"Okay," Anna nodded. And then, unable to think of much else to say: "Sorry."

On that, he burst out laughing, and fair enough. She tried to make eye contact with the barman, but he was right up at the other end.

"Like I said, I used to be acceptable."

"Right." Anna smiled. "And then what happened to you?"

"This place, actually. Want to hear about it?"

Anna paused. Even though he looked like he lived behind a chip shop, Danny was at least coherent. They were out in public, she could scream if he misbehaved. And in her experience, drunks love to tell a lengthy story. Hopefully that'd keep him talking long enough for Chloe to get here.

Not to mention: yes, he'd managed to get her just a little curious.

"Okay then," Anna nodded. "What happened?"

"I was in my late twenties in the early 2000s, you may not know what that was like – probably still at school. There were lots of bright-coloured shirts, hair gel. Not like nowadays, where being fashionable means dressing out of a skip.

Was as if the world only just discovered being shiny, y'know? So we were determined to glisten all the time, even if it made us look greasy. I was getting old, of course, late twenties and all, maybe that's why I didn't get into that.

In a damp-looking world, people try to moisten themselves out of age. The guys have smooth chests and rock-solid hair, the girls wear so much make-up, you can see your face in it.

Of course, you keep going to the cool bars, being a matte person just marks you out. You're a guy out in the club – sorry, *da club* – on a Friday night in the very early twenty-first century, you're not anyone if your hair doesn't stick at least an inch off your head.

But I already had a girlfriend, so who cares about clubbing anyway? Stephanie. She was ill. Doesn't matter how, really. She was ill. We lived together, because we both had enough of our families, and it was nice. She did a bit of work now and then, when she could, but I was doing the bulk of the earning.

I'd done bar work, I'd done office temp admin stuff, often-times I'd done both at once. This was pre-recession, y'know? Even when you were a drifting nobody, you could hit that magic sweet spot. Always enough work to go around, always paid enough to both cover the bills *and* go out every so often without feeling like you were stealing from your family.

Steph came out with me sometimes, it was alright. Worst comes to worst, you can just snog in the corner of the bar and people don't seem to care about your hair as much. Helped she was nice-looking, I suppose. People are shits, aren't they?

One day, I was in this pub we're in right now, The Left Hand, and it was what it is, you know? Long, thin, dirty. I was with some mates who were going on to a club and I'd just finished another run of temping. It hadn't gone well – it often didn't, at new places. I was just tired, you know? The end of my twenties, best years of my life according to some in the drunk community, and I just stopped caring.

Sometimes, when it's late at night and I'm drunk, I think about how that happened to me. Was it the shit jobs? The not-entirely-there relationship? Was I too young and restless to be the breadwinner? I dunno.

Anyway. I was in this place, and I needed money. Saw a bit of A4 stapled up behind the bar – before job vacancies went online, y'know – and gave them a shout. Funnily enough, since I had bar experience unlike the other great unwashed scum, I got the job without much trouble. Life was easy. People could get away with anything. But the real question is, Chloe, do you know what kind of place this is? Can you imagine what it used to be like back in the old days?"

"Of course, we didn't know how good we had it, did we? Whenever I came into this pub, it was rammed. Everyone had mad disposable income back then, but we're British, we still didn't want to spend it. Why have a big night out when you can go to your local cheapo chain pub and do beer and burger for a fiver?

Monday nights, cheap drinks. Thursday nights, cheap curry. Every night, cheap something. I loved it. Pub was always full, which hid the fact half the clientele were scumbags. But make no mistake, this is not a good place. People might overhear, so I hope you'll forgive my whispering.

I remember the day I realised. I'd been working here about three weeks, I was pretty into the rhythm. Broke a few glasses, everyone in the pub applauds like we're back at school, and you don't do it again. Never enjoyed that feeling of everyone looking at me.

I didn't have a day job and I wasn't a fucking failure, so I was already heading up the ranks. They were throwing so many shifts at me, I was almost ready to buy a new phone. Not a smartphone of course, we didn't have that shit yet, but I was well up for one of those hinged clam shell motherfuckers, y'know?

Sorry, you've managed to catch me just as I tip over the edge of drunk, and that's usually when the real swearing starts.

So one day in that third week, I got out of bed, kissed Steph, put my boring clothes on and went to sell pints to broke-down drunks. Because half the time during the day, that's all you get in here. A few lunch office twats, the occasional crowd of students and loads of mental pissheads.

We were much more open-minded about serving teenagers back then. After all, this was the early twenty-first century. Britain's town centres were dens of decadence, every cunt with a pub his own tin-pot Caligula. Whereas the youth of today gotta go to the park to drink pre-mixed gin and tonic in plastic wine glasses with milk-bottle tops. Poor little shits.

Right then, that day, I was working at the bar, pulling pints for people who probably had no liver, when the boss comes over to me. And this guy, Micro – you must've seen him if you've been in here at all, right? Massive bastard – huge guy. Bigger now than he was back then, but still, that one has never been thin. People blame the food here for him getting that size, but pretty sure it'd have happened anyway.

He expects us to put some effort in, but he's decent to work for as long as he doesn't think you're taking the piss. I was working the ale handle, trying to milk the last drops out, when Micro came over, rubbing against the bar as usual.

'Hey, Danny,' he said, 'just so you know, got some important guys coming in later. Serve them whatever they want, be charming, okay?'

'No worries, Micro,' I said, all smooth like, 'but how will I know them?'

'Group of men, mostly bald, mostly tracksuits. Let me know if you're not sure.'

There wasn't much doubt in the end. They turned up, about ten of them, looking fresh off the clone production line, if you know what I mean? Scary fuckers, Chloe. Scary.

They come up to the bar and they say: 'Pint of lager, please.' 'Pint of lager, please.' 'Pint of lager, please.' Again and again, same inflections, same five pound note, same slight European accent. I couldn't place it, so I didn't even try. Especially back then, easier to ignore anything foreign looking, treat them like everyone else. If you acknowledged it, you were probably being racist. And like I said, I was too tired to really care.

I served them all. There was one guy with a thin covering of hair, he spoke with a deeper accent and he was all: 'Be wanting a pint of lager, if you please.'

Weird. So I gave him his drink and smiled, Mr Hairy gave me this terrifying sneer in return, then he and his mates went into the corner. They were passing bags of white stuff around like they were tossing lettuce on a market stall. Turns out, The Left Hand was one of the only places in London where that happens, totally open. I mean, not so much nowadays. The old ways were too opulent for this shitty world.

Apparently there was a Left Hand discount where everything was half the street value. *Half!* I mean, get the feeling it was inferior product, but still, that's fucking weird.

So they came, settled in for a while, customers lined up by their booth, except pretending not to queue. Sat at the adjacent tables, always checking whether it was their turn yet. Every so often, someone looked over at me and I pretended to be cleaning something. Then I smashed a glass and got another round of applause. Didn't help me fade into the background, but still, they came and thanked me on the way out.

And that was how I first realised this place is the home of affordable commercial crime. Once you've seen it, all the subtle signs get obvious, y'know? One time, some woman with a bag over her head and rope around her hands got led through the bar to the back, but nothing huge, y'know?

Shit just happened. One time, my old temp agency called and offered me a new gig slinging paper in an office again. I should've said yes, obviously. Might've avoided a whole compost heap of bad stuff. But I didn't, because in a world where everyone was a greasy twat who did nothing so they could do nothing, this was interesting. I even started drinking in The Left Hand when I wasn't working, in case I saw something cool.

Once, I bumped into Mr Hairy, the leader of the bald drug squad, and he shook my hand and gave me a less scary smile. Then he said: 'My name is Joseph, hello.'

I told him my name, he said it was good to meet me and that was it. Steph was on a downturn in her health, so suited us both for me to keep busy. Fine as long as I was around for a quick sympathy shag when she felt better on weekend mornings.

I guess Micro and Joseph must've noticed I was on the scene a lot, taking an interest. One day, they came and offered me a little extra evening work."

"I'd had this sort of offer at other jobs – 'We've got a private function on, would you work it for a bit more money?'

In this case, it was after regular pub hours, starting at midnight, but that was fine for me as long as I had a decent nap that afternoon. Steph was just gonna be asleep anyway.

This being The Left Hand, it wasn't some company Christmas party. We shooed the pissed plebs out at eleven o'clock sharp, then started setting up. Nice network of tables off to the side, few sausages on sticks and pies, a straight passage through the middle to the beer garden, where the action was.

Micro was hustling around the kitchens, that was his domain. He shoved in and out of those flapping double doors every few minutes, wearing an apron that resembled a greased-up tent. He shouts, throws, looks like he might sit on you if you fuck with him. There were rumours they weren't just cooking food in the kitchens, there was big-time narcotics prep going on there. Might make sense, y'know? Might explain why there's a gleaming jungle of metal cylinders and pipes, but all the actual meals come from the microwave?

I don't know, though. I was never allowed in there. Micro was strict about who could spend any real time in the kitchen – I just took food from the heated shelf outside it. The guys who worked in there had tight white uniforms and shrivelled up faces, like cadavers or something. Zombie chefs!

I'm just fucking with you. Micro was strict, though. Like, when I tried to get into the kitchen because some dickhead was throwing a shitfit about their food, he damn near rugby tackled me. And a bodyslam from someone that size isn't a punch you forget. May just have been to stop me contaminating their product, but I like to think it was to save me from fucking myself up too.

Like, he really cared about me, you know? I still believe that. Even now, he gives me a smile when he walks past the table.

So, we had our garden party, some kinda drug cocktail cooking in the kitchen. Brief crisis when one of the games machines broke, bad too, but we did it. The first of Mr Hairy's guys turned up at midnight, and it turns out they'd asked for me specifically to work the bar. Felt good to know they liked me.

They came through, leading these dogs on leashes. I've never been a dog person, so I might not be the best guy to ask, but *fuck me.* Huge beasts, evil, salivating, most of them muzzled and going for their owners every step of the way. That's what was happening out back, of course – dog fighting. The animals slashed into each other, and any that died in the battles got cooked up and served on cheap steak night.

I hear that last part doesn't happen so much anymore – hygiene inspections, y'know?

My job was nothing to do with the dog fights out back – I barely even saw them, thankfully. Don't enjoy dogs, not a fan of extreme violence either. As far as I was concerned, simple bar gig. Served drinks, made conversation with the patrons – happily not many of them were scary bald clones – and kept the queue moving along.

Unsettling when someone comes into the bar with dog's blood smeared up to the knee, but that's part of the job. I think that's why I did well in that assignment, to be honest. Just looked at everything and thought: *Oh, it's that again.*

Not that bothered about what the fuck's going on, as long as I don't have to look at it. I can work the job, a tacit support staff co-conspirator, help your animal-maiming event run with a swing.

Looking back, maybe that was the problem with those days, you know? Willing to let anything go as long as we kept having a nice life. And the world fell apart because the government took the same approach with the bankers as I did with the scary Polish gangfucks. Whoops, shite, twiddly-dee, you know what I'm saying?

Maybe you don't, you're young.

Anyway, point is: I did a good job. They brought me in for the next few events and paid the shit out of me. I think sometimes they didn't read me right, though. They thought I liked the bad fuckery, thought I was one of them, when I was just bored and greedy. But that's probably just me trying to blame someone else for what happened next."

"So, in case you've not being paying attention to my thrilling fucking adventures, I became refreshments bitch to the criminal classes, while my girlfriend lay at home sick. Would any of this have happened if she hadn't been ill? I don't rightly know. Steph cared more about consequences, but she wasn't some kitten-hugging charity giver either.

So she wouldn't say *'Danny, stop doing crime, it's bad and wrong,'* but might've managed *'Danny, stop doing crime, it's dangerous.'* And as we're close to finding out, that second one was a fair point.

Doesn't matter, she didn't have a chance because I did all the crime while she was asleep. But one day, Steph woke up. She was on some new medication or something, managing her energy better. After a couple of months basically comatose, she was in the world again.

Since I was spending most of my spare time in The Left Hand at this point, I took her down there. Truth be told, I was so used to drug-passing, prisoner beating scumbaggery, I didn't realise how odd she'd find it.

Maybe I shouldn't have pointed everything out quite as gleefully, I admit.

Credit to her, she was fantastic. Chatted to Micro for a bit, did the mutual mockery thing people do when they meet through someone's boyfriend and pretend they're ganging up on him. It's annoying, but you can see why it happens.

So yeah, all great. Until we were left alone, and the inevitable happened.

I didn't tell her I'd turned down legal office work more than once in the last few weeks, I imagine that would've been the last straw. So Steph asked whether I could find something less crimey. Even if it paid less, she said, she'd be able to return to work soon, so it wouldn't matter.

So there we go. I could've made a decent excuse about making sure we had enough money, but she even ruined that for me. Selfish bitch.

You ever wish for something, then feel bad just for wanting it? And then the bad feeling never goes away, because the genie's out of the bottle. He floats around your head, threatening to grant your wish by existing.

I found myself thinking: wouldn't it be nice if she just stayed in her damn sickbed? I'd had such fun while she was asleep.

Didn't say that out loud, obviously. We were out in the pub, wasn't really the place. But I could feel it pressing at me, this lingering annoyance about her ruining my fun. Then she went for a piss and, again, didn't have a good phone to check because it was the fucking stone age. So I sat, clenched the old fists a bit.

Typically, that was when Mr Joseph Hairy popped in for a chat. In case I wasn't clear, Mr Hairy wasn't *that* hairy, it was a close-cropped style. But he insisted on hanging around with all these bald guys, so looked like a gorilla in comparison.

So, says Joseph, since I've been so okay with all the work so far, was I interested in coming with him the next day for something a bit more hands on? Nothing violent, he stressed, and the money was... well, let's just say not only does crime pay, it pays better than most temp jobs.

Well, fucked if I'm going to miss out on anything. Hell, if I'm about to be forced off this gig by Steph, might as well finish on a big one, you know?

Yes, I say. Abso-fucking-lutely. Sounds good."

"Now you're probably expecting me to say we ended up going on a hit or dealing drugs or whatever, but no, nothing so exciting. I wasn't suddenly some slick mafia wanker – remember, I didn't even use hair gel – I was a barman, and Mr Hairy wasn't an idiot. You don't take the refreshments jockey on a hit-and-run mission, unless you're a moron in a fucking terrible movie.

No, the gig was simple: a potential business associate was coming to town, offering him a cheap deal on something – you gotta assume drugs, but I wasn't dipshit enough to ask – and he was going to meet her to do intros, have a chat, negotiate terms.

My role? I was hospitality – take her coat, offer her drinks, show her where the pisser is, that sort of thing. Turns out, at this level of middle class crime, people expected a bit of the old luxury reception package. I guess it makes sense – especially back then.

Nowadays, get the feeling it's more scuzzy and clinical, those bells and whistles cost money. I was paid a *lot* for this, can't imagine they have the same cash to throw around on superficial shit nowadays. Plus, y'know, a lot of it has moved online and there's no wining and dining there. Just ones, zeros and pictures of fucking.

Apparently Mr Hairy didn't have a decent hospitality chap in his entourage. Made sense considering they were all photocopies of the same grumpy bald bloke. So he asked Micro for my services, and the big man was up for it. Even gave me paid time off for the evening without docking my holiday.

I rolled up that evening to meet Joseph, told Steph I was going to work as usual. I'd have been fucked if she decided to pop in and say hello. Based on her reaction the previous night though, I reckoned I was safe.

And the venue for this luxurious champagne reception? Why, it was the back office in The Left Hand, of course. So if Steph popped by, I could've always dashed out to greet her, though not sure Mr Hairy would look kindly on me shirking my duties.

I was at the bar, cleaning the big wine glasses specially. I'd gone out and bought a couple of good bottles of red – Micro refused to let our standard stuff be served to an important guest. I was also resisting the temptation to serve the building queue of customers. Christ, the kid filling in for me was a useless prick. Too busy growing new spots to pull any pints.

But Joseph, smile still thin and scary, said I should be ready to leap into action at any moment. No slipping away to do anything else – he'd taken me off Micro's payroll for the night so he could have my full attention. The meet-up was running half an hour late, but nonetheless, hardly my place to question the boss. So I cleaned the wine glasses for the fourth or fifth time.

It was coming up to nine o'clock, and I was torn between boredom and the smug feeling of being paid to do nothing. Was also a little chilly, because it was late and we were standing at the front of the pub, so got a blast of breeze every time the door opened. On Mr Hairy's insistence, I was wearing a suit jacket, which I'd smuggled into my bag to hide from Steph.

She would definitely have asked why I was dressing up so fancy to work in London's stickiest drinking hole. Every customer who entered the pub that night was thinking that. One or two even asked if the bar was closed for a private function. Joseph gave them a curt '*No!*' and demented glare until they got the message and fucked off.

Past nine and a couple of pissed kids were yelling '*Oi, penguin!*' at me. Just as I started to crack, Joseph's phone beep-beeped, and it was time.

'You are pouring the wine now,' he growled, pointing at the bar where the glasses sat, shining. I'd stopped washing them after the sixth or seventh round, for fear they might break. That'd piss Micro off.

Barely time to pick up the bottle and get two glasses poured, when the crappy doors to The Left Hand drifted open. So lightly, I thought it might be the wind, but it was her: *Vivia LaMorte.*

Now, Chloe, you might wonder whether that's her real name. I had the same thought myself, before I realised it was fucking moronic to even consider it.

Vivia LaMorte doesn't wear as much black as you'd expect. In fact, she ain't even that gothy – black nails, yeah, but aside from that, just a red shirt, grey jacket and trousers. The shirt is untucked, you notice as soon as you meet her. She is still wispy and dead-looking, though, which might be where she got the name.

Not important, anyway. Vivia wafted into the bar and I remembered the orders Joseph drilled into me. First thing to say: 'Can I take your jacket, Ms LaMorte?'

She shrugged it off and handed it to me, ignoring a couple of wolf-whistles from the arsehole armada up the bar.

'Joseph,' she gave him a scary smile, much like his own. 'Lovely to see you.'

Mr Hairy himself had abandoned his tracksuit and put on a jacket and tie. He would've looked handsome if not for the humming of evil.

'You also, Vivia. Would you like some wine?'

She nodded and I handed them both a glass, then Joseph indicated up the room. They walked stiffly past the bar, to the small door leading to the office. I followed, carrying her jacket and both wine bottles, taking great care not to spill the latter on the former.

There's a strange kick out of trailing along behind important people and disappearing into a private room, isn't there? I mean, God knows I was walking on air as I did it. For a few more minutes, at least."

"Once the chat started properly, it hit an odd note.

'I am admitting, Vivia,' Joseph says with a patronising smile, 'I was never seeing you as getting into the drugs. Whores, maybe, but not drugs.'

I don't pretend to be a mega-success with the ladies, but I'm not sure saying they'd make a lovely brothel madam will ever be a guaranteed vote-winner.

Vivia LaMorte didn't punch him, although I saw something in her eyes which suggested she'd quite like to. If only I'd paid more attention, eh?

Then again, what else would I *really* have done? That's the only way I've managed to live with everything: tell myself I would *never* have done anything other than what I did. And what did I do?

Exactly what I did in the rest of this story: nothing much. Stood idly by.

We were in Micro's office. I'd been in here before and it was never half this fucking tidy. Clearly whatever bung Mr Hairy slung his way was enough to make the big man catch up on his filing.

The certificates of managerial excellence and gourmet face-stuffing Micro won over the years were hung all over. Pictures of his surprisingly normal-sized family, paintwork glowing with white – he may even have cleaned the fucking walls.

Joseph took Micro's big-boss chair behind the desk, forced to perch on the end thanks to the epic arse-dent. Vivia sat on the guest seat opposite and lucky old Danny stood between them. They got straight down to business, without even bothering to send me outside. Did Joseph trust me with his operational secrets, or view me as such a worthless, terrified bumtick that he didn't care?

It's definitely the second one.

But, y'know, I wasn't there to be treated like a big man. I served wine whenever the glasses ran dry, not often as neither of them wanted to get tipsy, and they talked.

Vivia, it turned out, was into the drugs, but not in a skaggy way. 'Yes, Joseph, it's nice to finally deal with you as an equal, I must say.' Red flag number two. 'I hope we can do business together and put all the past messiness behind us.' And three.

Yeah, why didn't I run?

Even Joseph looked uncertain. 'Well, yes, that was all unpleasant. But let's be talking about what we are doing for each other now, yes?'

'Indeed.' She reached into her handbag. 'Let's be doing that.'

Viciously, the cow went for me first. I know I'm the one standing up holding a wine bottle, but surely she can tell I'm a decorative figurine in this meeting, and the dangerous criminal is Mr Hairy?

Apparently not. Vivia was holding a baton, a telescopic bit of rock hard plastic that expanded to twice the length of a police truncheon with one flick. The second movement sent it straight into my balls, which I didn't fucking enjoy, let me tell you.

I dropped the wine, terrified Micro would bollock me for wasting it, before she whacked me over the head. I wasn't knocked unconscious, because this isn't a TV show and Vivia isn't *that* strong. Still, I was lying down cupping myself long enough for her to give a similar treatment to Joseph. Then she zip-tied both our hands behind our backs, thankfully this time she did the actual crimelord first.

I don't know why it matters so much to have my essential uselessness acknowledged. Once again, I don't think it would've had much effect on how things worked out.

She locked us inside the room. Unluckily for myself and Mr Hairy, Micro had a quick-and-easy hand-operated lock fitted on his office door, stop any of us walking in while he was jerking himself dizzy to feeder porn.

So, in case you missed any details, me and Joseph were captured inside the main office of The Left Hand by a crazy woman named after both life and death. This, it goes without saying, was not what I signed up for."

"To my lasting fucking relief, Vivia kept her priorities in order. After doing my feet with another zip tie and gaffer-taping up my mouth, she shoved me in the corner to be forgotten. At last, I achieved the obscurity I'd longed for ever since the beatings started.

Then she crashed her handbag down on Micro's desk and pulled out a small metal bottle and a wicked curved knife. It wasn't even that big a bag, Chloe, so I don't fucking know how she fitted so much stuff into it. That woman was the Mary Poppins of torture.

I've had a decade to think up that smarty-pants description. My mind was elsewhere at the time – to be precise, the location was: '*AAAAARGGGHHHH AARGH OH MY GOD ARRRRRGHHH FUCKING AARRGH GOD SHIT ARRRRRGH!*' I believe you can find those co-ordinates on Google Maps.

But as I say, I was not the focus of her loving attentions. She gave me a look every so often, eyes dancing as if she enjoyed my gasping, choking horror.

Still, always clear who the main event was: Joseph.

Mr Hairy was as taped up as me, thrown over the arm of Micro's luxurious office chair like a naughty child. Unlike my good self, he wasn't trying to loosen his mouth-tape by hyperventilating against it. He kept his eyes staring, as if he wouldn't give her the satisfaction. I imagined his taped mouth still doing the smirk of victory, even as she grabbed her little hip flask and started unscrewing the lid.

'Joseph, old friend,' she smiled. 'I never thanked you enough, did I?'

He didn't waver, old Mr Hairy, whereas I was damn close to writing off my underwear. I guess that's why he's still in the game now, while I'm a broken husk of a cripple.

He only screamed against his tape when Vivia jerked the bottle. The smell of chemicals hit my nostrils an instant before the liquid splashed out over Joseph's head. After that, burning hair and scalp replaced it.

Why do I keep calling Joseph *Mr Hairy*, when to be honest, his hair is only a wee bit longer than all his mates? Real truth, Chloe, it's because this is my main memory of him. The image is burned into my mind almost as hard as that bottle of acid hissed and sizzled into his skull. Wasn't even too much, otherwise Joseph wouldn't have a brain.

But his hair was gone, roots and follicles fucked away to scabby ruin. His head looked like a red jellyfish. Vivia pulled the bottle away, unable to stop smiling as Joseph thrashed like a beached fish. The scream was audible through the gaffer tape, like a vacuum cleaner in another room.

'So, you sold me, you sold my friends and now you're fucked,' she said, as if he was in any state to listen.

Vivia twitched the bottle in her hand, as if weighing up whether to keep pouring and melt his entire head away. Back in my corner, I'd stopped huffing and held the air in my face tight. Waiting to see if I'd be next for a burn-out, or she'd slash my throat quickly at the end. Got the feeling I was only alive because she liked an audience.

So my heart jumped to another level when she grabbed the blade instead, leaving the bottle on the desk. Holding it to his throat, she reached to pull the tape away from his mouth. Just killing him wasn't enough – whatever she wanted to say to him, she had to hear him reply.

I couldn't relate to her at all in that moment, I realised. I'd never cared about something *that* badly.

But Vivia needed it. She waited through his initial roar of screaming pain, gesturing with the knife to indicate he should shut up. Once all fell quiet, she said it again, the same thing as before about her and her friends, as if it *deserved* a real reply. I suppose I'd done the same before when I'd made up a good joke.

And all he said, ice-calm considering his head was a raw bloody meat-sphere, was: 'Fuck you, bitch.'

Sticking to his fundamentals, even now. At a time when my first impulse would be to say whatever I thought she wanted to hear, anything to get out alive. Yeah, I kinda admired him.

Viciously disappointed, she pulled back her knife and whipped it into the side of his mouth. So bastard thin and sharp, it whistled into his flesh, leaving it to slide loose and bleed. His cheek flapped open in two oozing segments.

She laughed, he growled, the knife drew back.

They were both completely insane, egging each other on. The only way I was ever getting out of this alive was if I took positive action. As she concentrated on mutilating Mr Hairy, I rustled, pulled, tried to get some purchase. My wrists and ankles were tied together behind me as I lay face down, but Micro's office wasn't that big. If I kept my feet together without moving, I got my knees down to the ground soon enough. Then I strained my ankles harder to get myself up, muscles screaming up my stomach.

As I moved from the bottom of her field of vision to the top, Vivia finally turned from cutting holes in Joseph to look at me. She had a big knife, but the desk was between us. She'd also left the bottle of acid standing upright on the tabletop, without putting the lid back on.

Instead of trying to win a fight with all my limbs tied together, I lunged forward, smashing my entire unexercised bodyweight into the desk. It was cheap furniture from Ikea, so scraped easily along the floor. The acid bottle spilled and ran along the table towards her, forcing Vivia to jump away from Joseph.

Of course, the acid slick could have dissolved him away too, but I didn't care if they were both burnt to smears as long as I got away alive. Apathy, y'see?

Joseph was in an obvious storm of pain by now, but still with it enough to recognise an opportunity when it surged towards his face. He let himself fall back off the chair and kicked it towards Vivia. It smacked into her knees and doubled her over.

Now she didn't have a knife at his throat, Joseph felt free to do the one thing he could do in this situation: start fucking wailing. He screamed, he yelled, put his back into it, the pain in his head letting him method-act that screeching. I would've joined in if my mouth wasn't taped up.

Vivia must've figured the game was up now. Sure enough, after Mr Hairy sacrificed some dignity, two or three of his bald clone troopers appeared on the other side of the door, smacking away to get it open. The door wasn't standing up well, either – she knew she wouldn't have time to finish the job. So she clutched her knife and went to slash her way out.

I didn't see the resultant fight, but there was plenty of blood in the corridor afterwards. Sounded messy.

But right then, I was busy doing something stupid. I swiped the desk scissors from Micro's stationery holder and cutting the plastic ties holding myself and Joseph down. Took a minute to get the angle with my sodding hands tied together, but everyone outside was too busy bleeding to free us.

Joseph, never the most stable man in the world, turned and hissed at me as soon as I finished cutting him loose. I'd half-hoped my help in saving him would mean a handsome reward afterwards, but I'd reckoned without the sheer depth of his lunacy.

He seized the awful telescopic baton off Micro's desk, where Vivia had left it before getting to work with the knife and acid, and smashed me firmly around the face. Grabbed my neck before I could fall to the floor and threw me back against the wall, before beating me fucking senseless.

He used the thick handle of the baton to crack my kneecaps, then kicked them a few times until bloody white bone speared through my skin. Did the same to my elbows, whacked my shoulders until they cracked, punched me in the face until my nose bled out. After a while, I stopped even feeling individual blows, just drifted into a haze of red agony.

I couldn't see anymore. All I thought was: this isn't fair. This isn't the easy life I was promised. This is Steph's fault for not stopping me. This is my own fault for going along with too much.

Joseph drew his fist back for one last awful blow, like he was going to try and crush my entire skull, when Micro grabbed his hand from behind and wrenched the baton away. Joseph whirled around to go for him too, but Micro's a big guy. Commands a certain respect in the community. He told Joseph, in soft but clear tones, that he wouldn't be doing this shit in Micro's joint, and certainly not to the man himself.

Joseph hissed, stormed out, and Micro helped me get medical attention without going to jail. Told you he really cared about me."

"You know in those jokes or sitcoms, where a man tries to lie about something, unaware his clothes, body and general *self* are disproving his bullshit?

And yes, it is always a man.

'Sorry, honey, I couldn't get out of the office until late,' he says, with a brown smear of vomit stretching down the front of his coat, glistening with bits of carrot.

'Sweetie, of course I didn't sleep with her, I only have eyes for you,' he insists, unaware the other woman's knickers are still wrapped around his knee.

I might be a disinterested guy with no drive, but I'm not a fucking moron. 'Steph, of course I didn't get more involved with crime, I would never do that after you asked me not to,' was no longer an option. Not with all my limbs ground into horrible shapes, like a giant baby used me as a toy.

Like I say, I got treatment, my arms are okay bar a few shooting pains, I can even walk for a while if I gotta. I just choose not to most of the time, because fuck me, it hurts.

I still lied to her of course, just not about that. Said I was caught in the middle of some drunken crime-fight, but I wanted to keep working at The Left Hand and I didn't think it would work out between us. I'd love to say it was a heartbreaking, tearful moment, but no, mostly a relief.

Just to stress the scale of the lying: I didn't even keep working at The Left Hand. Eventually got a basic office job, although my newfound disability severely limited what I could take. Still, soon enough that recession happened, and then the rest of the world was just as hobbled as me.

Ah well, y'know? I'm still here in the pub. Because where the fuck else would I go where other people understand how I feel? We've all had different experiences, but end up broken in roughly the same way.

That's what these places are here for, I think. A safety net, a last resort. Yes, it's shit being a staring crazy drunk, but where else would I be? It is what it is. Let's all get on with it."

Anna wasn't sure what to say after that.

So she stayed silent, her long-empty drink in front of her. Danny sat back in his chair, looking proud to have shocked her quiet.

Hell, if his life was as empty as he claimed, maybe that made his day. Perhaps he lurked in this pub, searching out new excuses to tell his story and upset the shit out of people. Maybe it simply wasn't true –

after all, he was a crazy drunk in a pub. Why would his story be real?

"Well, thanks Danny," she said, at last.

"Y'welcome, sweetheart." He smiled, joyless. "It's shit, but it's *my* shit, you know what I mean?"

"Not really."

"Well, just don't repeat it to too many people. I'd hate anything bad to happen to you."

"Okay."

Anna was hit by the urge to run. Away from The Left Hand, maybe even from budget pubs altogether. Scramble back home, where she could drink alone, safe from Chloe's laziness.

"Well, nice talking to you," she said, smiling and getting to her feet. "Maybe see you around some time?"

"Sure thing, Chloe," he said, still only sounding amused.

She had no plans ever to come back here. He probably guessed.

As she rose, she saw a huge shape in a white apron clattering empty plates back to the kitchen. Micro? No, she told herself, it's all bullshit. Or he's thrown in one true detail to make it seem less like lies – after all, he spends so long in here, of course he knows the chef.

Patting her phone to make sure it was back in her pocket, Anna made her way to the front door. Needed to pee a little, but fucked if she was staying here to do it. Now she thought about it, weren't there a lot of similar-looking bald men in that corner?

Ignore them. Push on. Only a few more tables until she was free. The old men looked up as she passed, but only for a second before returning to their natural state of growling *"MotherFUCKERFUCK"* at the crossword.

She was past the tables. Her foot hit the edge of the scummy used-to-be-red doormat in front of the exit. This was it. Nearly out.

The door opened before she reached it, as weightless and free as Danny said.

Through the entrance came a man with a wicked scowl, a demented self-confidence, arrogant like some local king. His shirt was ruffled and untucked, but that didn't matter to him. Nor did the craggy moonscape of scarring all over his bald head, a few bursts of stubble sprouting through like stray weeds. On one side of his face, pulling tight as he smiled, was a scar that ran from the edge of his mouth, up his cheek.

The face turned on her.

Anna dropped her edgy calm and ran those last few steps, out of the door and down the street.

ACKNOWLEDGEMENTS

Since this is my first book to be published in any sense, it seems remiss not to thank people. On the other hand, since it's my first book, it's hard to resist the temptation to thank *everybody*. I'll try and keep it relevant.

From a practical perspective: huge appreciation to Gary at BubbleCow for his copyediting and Andrew & Rebecca at DesignForWriters for the cover design. If you need those services, check them out.

Thanks to everyone involved in Jukepop Serials, where the original *Hobson & Choi* webserial went up and found its first success. Much kudos to site masters Jerry and Jodi, the author community and every single reader. I doubly appreciate any of you who picked this book up despite having read the early draft online – hope you enjoyed the bonus story!

Not to mention the general webserial community, of course. I'd have been equally stuck without the help of the lovely people on Web Fiction Guide, both reviewers and forum commenters.

Also the Big Green Bookshop writing group - any and all of you. Your ongoing feedback and encouragement has been hugely important during this whole process.

Last of all: my Mum, without whom I'd never have started, and Leanne, without whom I'd never have finished.

ABOUT THE AUTHOR

Nick Bryan is a London-based writer of genre fiction, usually with some blackly comic twist. As well as the almighty detective saga *Hobson & Choi*, he is also working on a novel about the real implications of deals with the devil and has stories in several anthologies.

More details on his other work and news on future *Hobson & Choi* releases can be found online at **NickBryan.com** or on Twitter as **@NickMB.** Both are updated with perfect and reasonable regularity.

When not reading or writing books, Nick Bryan enjoys racquet sports, comics and a nice white beer.

Made in the USA
Charleston, SC
28 December 2014